kira-kira

kira-kira

CYNTHIA KADOHATA

ATHENEUM BOOKS FOR YOUNG READERS

New York   London   Toronto   Sydney

ATHENEUM BOOKS FOR YOUNG READERS

An imprint of Simon & Schuster Children's Publishing Division

1230 Avenue of the Americas, New York, New York 10020

This book is a work of fiction. Any references to historical events, real people, or real locales are used fictitiously. Other names, characters, places, and incidents are products of the author's imagination, and any resemblance to actual events or locales or persons, living or dead, is entirely coincidental.

Copyright © 2004 by Cynthia Kadohata

All rights reserved, including the right of reproduction in whole or in part in any form.

ATHENEUM BOOKS FOR YOUNG READERS is a registered trademark of

Simon & Schuster, Inc.

For information about special discounts for bulk purchases, please contact Simon & Schuster Special Sales at 1-866-506-1949 or business@simonandschuster.com.

The Simon & Schuster Speakers Bureau can bring authors to your live event. For more information or to book an event, contact the Simon & Schuster Speakers Bureau at 1-866-248-3049 or visit our website at www.simonspeakers.com.

Also available in a hardcover edition.

Book design by Ann Sullivan

The text for this book is set in Aldine401BT.

Manufactured in the United States of America

0419 OFF

First paperback edition December 2006

18 20 19

The Library of Congress has cataloged the hardcover edition as follows:

Kadohata, Cynthia.

Kira-Kira / Cynthia Kadohata.—1st ed.

p. cm.

Summary: Chronicles the close friendship between two Japanese-American sisters growing up in rural Georgia during the late 1950s, and the despair felt when one sister becomes terminally ill.

ISBN 978-0-689-85639-6 (hc)

[1. Sisters—Fiction. 2. Friendship—Fiction. 3. Japanese Americans—Fiction. 4. Death—Fiction. 5. Georgia—History—20th century—Fiction.] I. Title.

PZ7.K1166Ki 2004

[Fic]—dc21 2003000737

ISBN 978-0-689-85640-2 (pbk)

ISBN 978-1-4391-0660-0 (eBook)

For Kim

For Stan

And for Sara

acknowledgments

The author would like to thank her editor and friend, Caitlyn Dlouhy; George Miyamoto; Natalie and Miles Bergner and their father, Dan; Kim, Steve, and Caroline Maire; Keith Holeman; Jeannette Miyamoto; and Sonoko Sakai.

chapter 1

きらきら

My SISTER, LYNN, taught me my first word: *kira-kira*. I pronounced it *ka-a-ahhh*, but she knew what I meant. *Kira-kira* means "glittering" in Japanese. Lynn told me that when I was a baby, she used to take me onto our empty road at night, where we would lie on our backs and look at the stars while she said over and over, "Katie, say '*kira-kira, kira-kira.*'" I loved that word! When I grew older, I used *kira-kira* to describe everything I liked: the beautiful blue sky, puppies, kittens, butterflies, colored Kleenex.

My mother said we were misusing the word; you could not call a Kleenex *kira-kira.* She was dismayed over how un-Japanese we were and vowed to send us to Japan one day. I didn't care where she sent me, so long as Lynn came along.

I was born in Iowa in 1951. I know a lot about when I was a little girl, because my sister used to keep a diary. Today I keep her diary in a drawer next to my bed.

I like to see how her memories were the same as mine, but also different. For instance, one of my earliest memories is of the day Lynn saved my life. I was almost five, and she was almost nine. We were playing on the empty road near our house. Fields of tall corn stretched into the distance wherever you looked. A dirty gray dog ran out of the field near us, and then he ran back in. Lynn loved animals. Her long black hair disappeared into the corn as she chased the dog. The summer sky was clear and blue. I felt a brief fear as Lynn disappeared into the cornstalks. When she wasn't in school, she stayed with me constantly. Both our parents worked. Officially, I stayed all day with a lady from down the road, but unofficially, Lynn was the one who took care of me.

After Lynn ran into the field, I couldn't see anything but corn.

"Lynnie!" I shouted. We weren't that far from our house, but I felt scared. I burst into tears.

Somehow or other, Lynn got behind me and said, "Boo!" and I cried some more. She just laughed and hugged me and said, "You're the best little sister in the world!" I liked it when she said that, so I stopped crying.

The dog ran off. We lay on our backs in the middle of the road and stared at the blue sky. Some days nobody at all drove down our little road. We could have lain on our backs all day and never got hit.

Lynn said, "The blue of the sky is one of the most special colors in the world, because the color is deep but see-through both at the same time. What did I just say?"

"The sky is special."

"The ocean is like that too, and people's eyes."

3

She turned her head toward me and waited. I said, "The ocean and people's eyes are special too."

That's how I learned about eyes, sky, and ocean: the three special, deep, colored, see-through things. I turned to Lynnie. Her eyes were deep and black, like mine.

The dog burst from the field suddenly, growling and snarling. Its teeth were long and yellow. We screamed and jumped up. The dog grabbed at my pants. As I pulled away, the dog ripped my pants and his cold teeth touched my skin. "Aaahhhhh!" I screamed.

Lynn pulled at the dog's tail and shouted at me, "Run, Katie, run!" I ran, hearing the dog growling and Lynnie grunting. When I got to the house, I turned around and saw the dog tearing at Lynn's pants as she huddled over into a ball. I ran inside and looked for a weapon. I couldn't think straight. I got a milk bottle out of the fridge and ran toward Lynn and threw the bottle at the dog. The bottle missed the dog and broke on the street. The dog rushed to lap up the milk.

Lynn and I ran toward the house, but

she stopped on the porch. I pulled at her. "Come on!"

She looked worried. "He's going to cut his tongue on the glass."

"Who cares?"

But she got the water hose and chased the dog away with the water, so it wouldn't hurt its tongue. That's the way Lynn was. Even if you tried to kill her and bite off her leg, she still forgave you.

This is what Lynn said in her diary from that day:

> The corn was so pretty. When it was all around me, I felt like I wanted to stay there forever. Then I heard Katie crying, and I ran out as fast as I could. I was so scared. I thought something had happened to her!
> Later, when the dog attacked me, Katie saved my life.

I didn't really see things that way. If she hadn't saved my life first, I wouldn't have been able to save her life. So, really, she's the one who saved a life.

Lynn was the bravest girl in the world. She was also a genius. I knew this because one day I asked her, "Are you a genius?" And she said, "Yes." I believed her because the day my father taught her how to play chess, she won her first game. She said she would teach me how to play if I wanted. She always said she would teach me everything in the world I needed to know. She said we would be rich someday and buy our parents seven houses. But first they would buy a house for all of us. That wonderful day was not far off. I found this out one afternoon when Lynn pulled me into the kitchen, her eyes shining. "I have to show you something," she said.

She reached under the refrigerator and pulled out a tray. A worn envelope sat inside. She opened the envelope up and showed me what was inside: cash.

"Is that real?" I said.

"Uh-huh. It belongs to Mom and Dad. It's for our house we're going to buy."

We lived in a little rented house in Iowa. I

liked our little rented house, but Lynn always told me I would *love* our very own house. Then we could get a dog, a cat, and a parakeet.

Lynn looked at me expectantly. I said, "Doesn't money belong in a bank?"

"They don't trust the bank. Do you want to count it?"

She handed me the envelope, and I took the money in my hands. It felt damp and cool. "One, two, three . . ." I counted to eleven. Eleven hundred-dollar bills. I wasn't sure what to think. I found a dollar once in a parking lot. I bought a lot of stuff with that. With eleven hundred dollars, it seemed you could buy anything. "I hope our house is painted sky blue," I said.

"It will be." She put the money back. "They think it's hidden, but I saw Mom take it out."

Our parents owned a small Oriental foods grocery store. Unfortunately, there were hardly any Oriental people in Iowa, and the store went out of business shortly after Lynn and I first counted the money under the refrigerator. My father's brother, my uncle

Katsuhisa, worked in a poultry hatchery in Georgia. He said he could get my father a job at the hatchery. And, he said, he could get my mother a job working in a poultry processing factory. A few weeks after the store went out of business, my father decided to take us down to Georgia to join the poultry industry.

So we owed Uncle Katsuhisa a big favor for helping us. *Katsu* means "triumph" in Japanese. For some reason I always thought "triumph" and "trumpet" were the same thing, and I thought of my uncle as a trumpet.

Lynn said Uncle Katsuhisa was an odd fish. He was as loud as my father was quiet. Even when he wasn't talking, he made a lot of noise, clearing his throat and sniffing and tapping his fingers. Sometimes, for no reason that I could see, he would suddenly stand up and clap his hands together really loudly. After he got everyone's attention, he would just sit down again. He even made noise when he was thinking. When he was deep in thought, he had a way of turning his ears inside out so they looked kind of deformed. The ears would make a popping sound when they came undone. Lynn said you could hear him thinking: *Pop! Pop!*

A buttonlike scar marked one side of Uncle Katsuhisa's nose. The story was that when he was a boy in Japan, he was attacked by giant crows, one of which tried to steal his nose. He, my father, and my mother were *Kibei*, which meant they were born in the United States but were sent to Japan for their education. The crows of Japan are famous for being mean. Anyway, that was the story Lynn told me.

It was a sweltering day when Uncle Katsuhisa arrived in Iowa to help us move to Georgia. We all ran outside when we heard his truck on our lonely road. His truck jerked and sputtered and was generally as noisy as he was. My mother said, "Will that truck make it all the way to Georgia?"

My father hit his chest with his fist. That's what he did whenever he wanted to say, *Definitely!* He added, "He's my brother." Our father was solid and tall, six feet, and our mother was delicate and tiny, four feet ten. As tiny as she was, she scared us when she got mad. Her soft face turned hard and glasslike, as if it could break into pieces if something hit it.

As my parents watched Uncle's truck, my father reached both of his arms around my mother, enveloping her. He stood with her like that a lot, as if protecting her.

"But his being your brother has nothing to do with whether the truck will make it all the way to Georgia," my mother said.

My father said, "If my brother says it will make it, then it will make it." He didn't seem to have a doubt in the world. His brother was four years older than he was. Maybe he trusted Uncle Katsuhisa the way I trusted Lynn. Lynn whispered to me, "Frankly, I wonder whether the truck will make it all the way up the road to our house, let alone to Georgia." "Frankly" was her favorite word that week.

Our mother looked at us suspiciously. She didn't like it when we whispered. She thought that meant we were gossiping, and she was against gossiping. She focused on me. She was trying to read my mind. Lynn said whenever our mother did that, I should try to think nonsense words in my head. I thought to myself,

Elephant, cow, moo, koo, doo. Elephant . . . My mother turned back around, to watch the truck.

When the truck finally rumbled up, Uncle Katsuhisa jumped out and immediately ran toward Lynn and me. I stepped back, but he swooped me up in his arms and shouted, "My little palomino pony! That's what you are!" He twirled me around until I felt dizzy. Then he set me down and picked up Lynn and twirled her around and said, "My little wolfie girl!"

He set Lynn down and hugged my father hard. He hugged my mother delicately. While Uncle hugged my mother, she turned her face away a bit, as if his loudness made her feel faint.

It was hard to see how my father and Uncle Katsuhisa could be related. My father was mild, like the sea on a windless day, with an unruffled surface and little variation. He was as hard as the wall in our bedroom. Just to prove how strong he was, he used to let us hit him in the stomach as hard as we could. Some days we would sneak up on him and punch him in the stomach, and he never even noticed. We would sneak away while he kept listening to the radio as if nothing had happened.

My father liked to think. Sometimes Lynn and I would peek at him as he sat at the kitchen table, thinking. His hands would be folded on the table, and he would be frowning at nothing. Sometimes he would nod, but only slightly. I knew I would never be a thinker like my father, because I couldn't sit that still. Lynn said he thought so much that sometimes weeks or even months passed before he made a decision. Once he decided something, though, he never changed his mind. He'd thought many weeks before deciding to move us to Georgia. By the time he decided, there was only six hundred dollars in cash left in the envelope under the refrigerator.

The night Uncle Katsuhisa arrived in Iowa, he left the dinner table early so he could go out and take a walk and maybe talk to himself. After the front door closed, my mother said that Uncle Katsuhisa was the opposite of my father in that he didn't look before he leapt, didn't think at all before he made decisions. She lowered her voice and said, "That's why he married that woman," meaning his first wife. Strictly speaking, Mom was gossiping, but who was going to tell her? We all sat silently.

My father and uncle were different in other ways. Uncle Katsuhisa liked to talk to anyone, even to himself. My father didn't like to talk, except to my mother. He preferred to read the newspaper. My uncle, on the other hand, never read the paper. He did not give a hoot what President Eisenhower had to say.

My uncle was exactly one inch taller than my father. But his stomach was soft. We knew this because we hit him in it once the year before, and he yelped in pain and threatened to spank us. We got sent to bed without supper because my parents said hitting someone was the worst thing you could do. Stealing was second, and lying was third.

Before I was twelve, I would have committed all three of those crimes.

chapter 2 きらきら

ALL THE DAY before we moved, my father and uncle loaded the truck with boxes that my mother had packed. We planned to leave first thing the next morning. Lynn and I sat out on the front porch and watched them work. Uncle Katsuhisa didn't want us to help because he said we got in a man's way.

Lynn and I played soldier with the chess set. During a break, Uncle Katsuhisa walked onto the porch, clapped his hands three times, took out a handkerchief, and blew his nose. He clapped his hands again. "I'm the best Japanese chess player I know," he said. That was a challenge to Lynn. "Are you up to a game?"

She set up the board. He rolled up his sleeves, as if chess were hard, physical work. Lynn beat him in about fifteen minutes. He was not a good sport and made her play him again and again so he could beat her. My father returned to loading up the truck, but Uncle Katsuhisa didn't even notice. He lost three games! He said again that he thought of himself as the best Japanese chess player in the whole United States. I have no idea where he got that idea of himself. When Lynn beat him, I kept my face blank, but inside I was cheering for her.

After Uncle's third loss he stepped off the porch and stared moodily across the gravel yard. He started making noises in his throat. He said, "Yah! Ooo-YAH! Gaaaaaaah! Gaaaaaaaah! Gaaaaaaah! Hocka-hocka-hocka! Geh-geh-geh-geh-geh!!" And then a glob of saliva flew like a baseball from his mouth and over the gravel. It landed on our only tree and dripped slowly down the bark. Lynn and I looked at each other, and she raised her eyebrows as if to say, *See, I told you he was an odd fish.*

We were poor, but in the way Japanese are poor, meaning we never borrowed money from anyone, period. Meaning once a year we bought as many fifty-pound bags of rice as we could afford, and we didn't get nervous again about money until we reached our last bag. Nothing went to waste in our house. For breakfast my parents often made their *ochazuke*—green tea mixed with rice—from the crusty old rice at the bottom of the pot. For our move to Georgia, Dad and Uncle loaded up the truck with all the bags of rice that we hadn't sold at the store. I watched my parents look at the rice in the truck, and I could see that the rice made them feel good. It made them feel safe.

I liked to see them that way, especially my mother, who never seemed to feel safe. My mother was a delicate, rare, and beautiful flower. Our father told us that. She weighed hardly more than Lynn. She was so delicate that if you bumped into her accidentally, you could bruise her. She fell down a single stair once, and she broke her leg. To her that was proof even a single stair could present peril. When I would approach even a single stair, she would call out, "Be careful!"

Our mother didn't like us to run or play or climb, because it was dangerous. She didn't like us to walk in the middle of our empty street, because you never knew. She didn't want us to go to college someday, because we might get strange ideas. She liked peace and quiet. My father used to say, "Shhhh. Your mother is taking a bath." Or, "Quiet down, girls, your mother is drinking tea." We never understood why we couldn't make noise while our mother was doing anything at all. My mother's favorite thing to tell us, in her iron-rimmed singsong voice, was *"Shizukani!"* That means "Hush!"

She never said *"Shizukani!"* to my father. She made him food and rubbed his feet, and for this he let her handle all the money. Lynn said our mother probably knew a special foot-rubbing technique that made men silly. My father loved my mother a lot. That made *me* feel safe.

The night before we moved, my father and

uncle sat on a tree stump across the road. Lynn and I peeked out at them before we got in bed. My uncle talked and talked, and my father listened and listened. Sometimes they both laughed loudly.

"What are they talking about?" I said.

"Women," Lynn said knowingly.

"What are they saying about women?"

"That the pretty ones make them giggle."

"Oh. Good night."

"Good night!"

Our mother came into the bedroom in the middle of the night, the way she always did, to make sure we were asleep. As usual, Lynn was asleep and I was awake. If I was awake, I usually pretended to be asleep so as not to get in trouble. But tonight I said, "Mom?"

"It's late, why are you up?"

"I can't sleep without Bera-Bera." Bera-Bera was my favorite stuffed animal, which my mother had packed in a box. Bera-Bera talked too much, laughed too loudly, and sometimes sassed me, but still I loved him.

"Someday you won't even remember Bera-Bera." She said this gently, and as if the thought made her a little sad. The thought made me a little sad too. She kissed my forehead and left. Outside I could hear noises: "Yah! Ooooh-YAH!" Et cetera. Lynn was sound asleep. I got up and watched Uncle Katsuhisa spit. My father no longer sat on the tree stump. It was just Uncle Katsuhisa out there. He was a madman, for sure.

We left Iowa at dusk the next evening. We had meant to leave in the morning but got a little behind schedule for several reasons:

1. I couldn't find the box with Bera-Bera, and I was convinced he was lost. Naturally, I had to have hysterics.
2. My parents misplaced their six hundred dollars.
3. Lynn couldn't find her favorite sweater with embroidered flowers. Naturally, she had to have hysterics.
4. Uncle Katsuhisa fell asleep, and we thought it would be rude to wake him.

Uncle woke up on his own. My parents found their money. But Lynn and I didn't find our items, so naturally, we continued our hysterics. Finally, my mother said, "We must leave or I don't know what!" She looked at Lynn and me crying. "Maybe you girls should keep your uncle company while he drives."

"Oh, no," said Uncle. "I wouldn't want to deprive you of their delightful company."

"No," said my mother. "I wouldn't want you to be lonely."

So we climbed into the noisy truck with our noisy uncle. Then we cried so much that our uncle refused to drive with us anymore. He pulled to the side of the highway. Then we got in our parents' car and cried so much that they pulled over and flipped a coin with Uncle Katsuhisa. Uncle lost, so we got back in the truck with him.

Lynn and I were perfectly happy in Iowa. I did not see why we had to move to a new job that my father had told us would be the hardest work he had ever done. I did not see why we had to move to a southern state where my father said you could not understand a word people said because of their southern accents. I did not see why we had to leave our house for a small apartment.

After awhile Lynn and I ran out of tears and sat glumly in the truck with Uncle Katsuhisa. I knew if I thought of Bera-Bera, I would cry. But I had nothing else to do, so I thought of him. He was half dog, half rabbit, and he had orange fur. He was my best friend next to Lynn. "I want Bera-Bera!" I cried out.

Lynn cried out, "I want my sweater!" We both burst into tears.

It was a warm night. Whenever we paused in our crying, the only other sound inside the truck was the sound of my uncle smacking his chewing tobacco. I dreaded to know what would happen when he spit out that tobacco. Now he rolled down the window, and I thought the Great Spit was about to come. Instead, he looked at us slyly.

"I could teach you girls how to spit like a master," he said.

My sister squinted at him. She stopped crying. So did I. I could tell she thought it might be fun to learn how to spit like a master. So did I. Our mother would kill us. Lynn said, "Maybe."

He belched very loudly, then glanced at us. I realized his belch was preparation for spitting. I swallowed some air and burped. So did Lynn. Then Uncle Katsuhisa's throat rumbled. The rumbling got louder and louder. Even over the sound of the motor, it seemed like a war was going on in his throat. Lynn and I tried to rumble our throats like him.

"Hocka-hocka-hocka!" he said.

Lynn and I copied him: "Hocka-hocka-hocka!"

"Geh-geh-geh!"

"Geh-geh-geh!"

He turned to his open window, and an amazing wad of brown juice flew from his mouth. The brown juice was like a bat bursting out of a cave. We turned around to watch it speed away. A part of me hoped it would hit the car behind us, but it didn't. I leaned over Lynn and out the passenger window. "Hyaaahhhh!" I said, and a little trickle of saliva fell down my chin.

No one spoke. For some reason the silence made me start crying again. As if Uncle Katsuhisa couldn't restrain himself, he started singing my name over and over, "Katie, Katie, Katie . . ." Then he sang Katie songs to the tunes of "Row, Row, Row Your Boat," "America the Beautiful," "Kookaburra," and some songs I didn't recognize. For instance, he sang, "Oh, Katie, Kate, for spacious skies, for Katie Katie Kate." He made me giggle. It was almost as if someone were tickling me. For a while I forgot about Bera-Bera.

Lynn smiled with satisfaction. I knew this was because she liked for me to be happy. The wind hit our hair as Uncle Katsuhisa continued to sing Katie songs. I looked outside over a field and tried to find the *Sode Boshi,* the kimono sleeve in the sky where Uncle Katsuhisa said westerners see the constellation Orion. Then my uncle began to sing Lynnie songs.

She laughed and laughed and laughed.

chapter 3

きらきら

WE DROVE THROUGH two big cities: St. Louis, Missouri, and Nashville, Tennessee. In St. Louis the grown-ups left us in the car while they bought necessities. We watched them walk away toward a store. Then we got out to explore.

We walked to the next block, to look at a building that was five stories tall. It was the highest building I'd ever seen.

"There are buildings in Chicago more than ten times higher," said Lynn.

"Are you sure?"

"Yup. Maybe fifteen times."

I thought the building was ugly, but her eyes shone brightly. Lynn's eyes were often *kira-kira*. "When we go to college, we're not going to live in a dormitory. We're going to live on the very top floor of a tall apartment building. I'll be in graduate school." Lynn planned to become either a rocket scientist or a famous writer. Though I knew nothing about animals, she said that when I grew up I would go to Africa and study them. I can't say that the idea of college was foremost on my mind; nevertheless, if Lynn was going, I would too.

We walked back to the car and sat on the hood and swung our legs, like the women in our former town who my mother said were floozies. We pretended to smoke cigarettes like the floozies. But we got back in the car before our mother returned, because if she saw us looking like floozies, it might make her so upset that she would need to take an aspirin. Then our father would worry and he might not drive as well and they would get in an accident and get killed. That's why, even though I liked being bad all the time, I tried hard to be good.

We rode with our parents for a while after that. They didn't talk for two whole hours. Then we got back in the truck with our uncle, and he never stopped talking. In Nashville we temporarily lost our parents because Uncle turned down a side street when he spotted a pawnshop. He pulled over, and we waited while he went inside. When he came out, he showed us a marble chess set he'd bought. He said that it had cost him an arm and a leg and that it was now his lucky chess set. He asked me if I thought he could beat Lynn with this lucky set, and I said no. My mother always told me to be polite, but, of course, she also said lying was one of the worst things you could do. So I chose to tell the truth to my uncle. Lynn said that sometimes in life you had to make choices.

We stopped somewhere called the Country Bear Motel across the street from the bus station. My father let me come with him to get a room. When we got into the office, a tall woman was laughing into a phone. Her hair was mostly as black as mine, with an inch of white roots. She ignored us, so we waited.

I kept looking at my dad to see whether he was going to try to hurry her along. But he was the most patient man in the world.

"You have got to be kidding, honey," the woman said into the phone. "He said that?! You should have slapped his face right then and there!" My father counted the bills in his wallet. She moved her mouth from the phone and said to my father, "Indians stay in the back rooms." She pushed a key and a registration card toward my father.

"We're not Indian," I said.

"Mexicans, too." My father was dark that summer from working in the backyard.

"We're not Mexican," I said. If my mother had been there, she would have made me quiet down. But my father just quietly filled out the registration card.

The woman spoke into the phone. "Hold on a second, hon." She set the receiver down and turned her full focus on me. I took hold of my father's hand. "Young lady, look at me."

Finally, my father spoke. "A back room is fine," he said.

"I just want to ask the girl something.

Now, I'm serious, girl, because I've had a lot of trouble in my life, and I just want to know: Is there something on my forehead that spells 'I like trouble'? Does my face say to people, 'Trouble is my friend'? I'm asking you seriously."

I concentrated on the woman's face. I glanced at my father, but he was studying the woman's forehead.

The woman continued, "Are my veins shaped like a 'T' for 'trouble'?"

She did have some veins on her forehead. But they didn't look like a "T" really. So I said, "No, ma'am."

"I didn't think so. Now you all go to your room." She picked up the phone again. My father left some money, and she looked up again. "Back rooms are two dollars extra." My father slid another two dollars across the counter.

The woman picked up the phone and listened a moment. "Shhhheee-it! You put up with too much from that man!"

We walked outside into the placid evening. The sun was setting and the horizon was tangerine. Disk-shaped clouds hung in the sky.

"What's 'shhheee-it'?" I said.

My father leaned over and whispered in my ear what it was. He used the Japanese word, which, naturally, Lynn had already taught me. "Whatever you do, don't tell your mother I told you that."

"I won't. One of her veins did sort of look like a 'T.' It wasn't on her forehead. It was on her cheek."

"Looked like a 'B' to me, but I won't tell you what that stands for."

"What? What what what? Tell me what it stands for!"

My father looked around, as if he thought my mother might suddenly appear. Then he leaned over and whispered in my ear what "B" stood for. He said it stood for "bad lady."

"If she's so bad, how come you gave her two dollars extra?"

"Because you need a place to sleep," he said.

"You could have beat her up," I said.

He picked me up in his strong arms and didn't reply.

When we got to our room, we saw some

real Indians sitting on the curb. They looked at us as if they had never seen anything quite like us, and we looked at them the same way.

Japan had people like Indians too. They were called the Ainu. My uncle had told Lynn and me about the Ainu. They were the first people ever to live in northern Japan. The Ainu called themselves the Sky People because they said their ancestors came from the sky, just like my ancestors came from Tokyo. The Ainu females used to tattoo mustaches on their faces. Lynn and I thought that sounded pretty. After our uncle told us about the Ainu, we painted mustaches on our faces every day for two weeks. Our father took pictures. Our mother got so upset, she had to lie down. She did not think of Japan as the land of Ainu, but rather as the land of her parents and the land where Lynn and I would eventually get sent to learn our femininity. My mother did not think mustaches were feminine. I don't know why.

That night in the motel Uncle Katsuhisa didn't challenge Lynn to a game right away. First he took the chess set into the bathroom and closed the door. We heard him mumbling to himself. When I had to pee, he ignored my knocking, probably because he was concentrating so hard. Lynn had to take me to the motel office and ask to use their bathroom. The Evil Vein Lady was there. She didn't say anything, just shook her head in annoyance and handed us the key. Her head swayed, as if she could hardly keep it up. Lynn whispered to me, "She's drunk, I'm not gossiping, just explaining the facts." The woman's head fell to the counter. Earlier I hadn't liked her, but now I felt bad for her. I wondered if her parents loved her as much as mine loved me.

When we returned to our room, Uncle Katsuhisa was ready to challenge Lynn. They sat down at the small table in our room. I sat on the bed with Bera-Bera and watched the game. My father had spent an hour searching through the truck for Bera-Bera and my sister's sweater.

Uncle made a big show of clearing his throat. Then he thought and thought. He popped his ears twenty-seven times—I counted. It took him about ten minutes to move one

31

pawn! I would have been bored, but Bera-Bera talked to me all the time. He told me everything he did every day. All he did was talk. He also talked to Lynn. He told her that he knew Alice from the *Through the Looking Glass* book and that, like Alice, he could enter the magic world of reflections. When you looked at a clear reflection, like in a pond or a mirror, the reflection looked almost exactly like the real thing. But the world of reflections was different—it was magic. Naturally, Lynn had taught me that. She told me that Bera-Bera had many friends in the magic world of reflections. In his other world he was very important—maybe he was even emperor—but with me he was just my loving, talkative friend.

Lynn took about two seconds to move a pawn. Uncle Katsuhisa took about fifteen minutes to move another pawn. Then Lynn moved a knight, and Uncle Katsuhisa looked stunned. I fell asleep, and when I woke up, Lynn was slumping in her chair looking bored. Uncle was frowning, deep in thought. Lynn still had her queen and he didn't. For a moment I thought Uncle was going to cry.

Then he tipped over his king—that meant he surrendered. He walked outside, and we ran to the window to watch him spit. He was kind of like the geyser our father took us to see once at Yellowstone. That is, he spit at regular intervals. The Indians were sitting outside again. They looked at Uncle as if he might possibly be losing his mind.

"Should I let him win one time?" said Lynn.

"No," I said.

That night, when I woke up in the middle of the night, I noticed a crack of light under the bathroom door. Uncle's cot was empty. I knew he was studying his chessboard. I felt a little sorry for him. He probably wanted to be a genius like Lynn. Maybe he envied her bright future.

Sometimes I thought about my future, because Lynn said I should. She said it was hard to tell at this point, but someday, if I didn't go to Africa to study animals, I might be a beautiful genius tennis player. I didn't worry about it one way or another. I didn't care if I was a genius or if I was pretty or if I was good in sports. I just liked to listen to Lynn and to talk to Bera-Bera and to eat rice candies. The lady who used to live down the street could take all of her top teeth out of her mouth. She wasn't allowed to eat chewy candy. I could eat any kind of candy I wanted because I still had my baby teeth. If they rotted, I would simply grow more teeth. That was pretty great.

From the car Georgia didn't seem so different from anyplace else. But when we got out of the car and talked to people, we couldn't understand them because of their southern accents. They talked like their mouths were full of rubber bands! People stared at us when we went into their restaurants. The restaurant signs said things like COLORED IN BACK. The white people sat at the front. We didn't know where to sit, so we always ordered to-go. We didn't see another Japanese person anywhere. We got stared at quite a bit. Sometimes a white lady would lean over us and exclaim, "How cute!" Some of them touched our faces, as if they weren't sure we were real.

Georgia had many claims to fame. During

our driving Lynn read me all the signs: GORDON, CHICKEN CAPITAL OF THE WORLD; VIDALIA, HOME OF THE SWEETEST ONIONS IN THE WORLD; CORDELE, WATERMELON CAPITAL OF THE WORLD; MILTON, THE WORLD'S BEST PEACHES; and TEMPLETON, WHERE PEANUTS ARE KING. We also saw seven different restaurants that claimed to have the world's best BBQ.

Several times we drove by an antebellum mansion. "Antebellum" means "before the Civil War." Lynn taught me that. She had tried to read the whole dictionary once, so she knew the definitions of a lot of words that started with "a." An antebellum mansion was not as beautiful as, say, a mountain or the sky, but for a house it was pretty darn nice. Before the Civil War really rich white people lived in the mansions and owned slaves. I didn't know who lived in them now.

Our new town was called Chesterfield. Uncle told us the population was 4,001. Six other Japanese families lived in Chesterfield. Including us, that made a grand total of thirty-one Japanese people. All of the fathers worked at the hatchery in a nearby town.

We had ridden most of the day in the truck with our uncle because he wanted to talk chess with Lynn. I mostly just stared out the window the whole time. Shortly before we arrived in Chesterfield, I took a nap. When I woke up, I saw I had wet my pants. I didn't tell Lynn or my uncle. We were going to Uncle's house, where he planned to throw a little welcome party for us that night. I thought maybe I could sneak inside his house without anybody noticing. We rolled down a curvy road. Here and there I saw a small frame house with chipping paint. Old rusted cars or piles of tires sat in the yards. Chickens ran loose. We saw a dead chicken in the road, and Lynn and I screamed. Finally we stopped at a small house just like all the others.

Uncle Katsuhisa's family came out to greet us. He was the only Japanese in town who owned a house. The front yard was composed of gravel with bits of yellow grass, and the paint on the house was chipped. Still, it seemed okay to me. My own family would be living in the same cheap apartment building as the other Japanese who worked at the hatchery. Uncle Katsuhisa lived in a house because he was different. He had big plans. First of all, he had inherited two thousand dollars from a man whose life he'd saved during World War II. So while he wasn't rich, he was better off than most of us. Second of all, he was studying with a friend to work as a land surveyor, which is where you measure and study land. He knew a lot about soil and mud and things like that. He did not want to work in a hatchery all his life.

When we arrived at his house, my six-year-old twin cousins, David and Daniel, were waiting with Auntie Fumiko. Auntie was a round woman, with a round face, round tummy, and round calves. Even her hair was shaped into a big round thing on her head. Someday I planned to knock it over and see what was inside it. Uncle popped his horn and waved at them. We got out of the car, and almost the first thing that happened was my auntie Fumi started shouting at the top of her lungs, "Katie wet herself! Katie wet herself!" I was so embarrassed that I burst into tears. Everybody laughed, and David and Daniel shouted out, "Katie wet herself!" My mother said, "Katie wet herself!" My father looked proud of me. He was proud of us no matter what we did.

Later, when the other Japanese families arrived, we ate all night long: salted rice balls, fish cakes, rice crackers, rice candies, and barbecued chicken. Rice balls are called *onigiri*, and they were the only thing I knew how to make. To make *onigiri*, you wash your hands and cover your palms with salt. Then you grab a handful of rice and shape it into a lump. My mother made fancy triangle-shaped *onigiri*, with seaweed and pickled plums, but I just made the basic kind. Someday when I got older, I would have to learn to make fancy *onigiri* too, or nobody would marry me.

We picked fruit off a peach tree nearby and listened to our parents talk about business. My father would be working as a chicken sexer, which he told us is where you separate the male chicks from the female chicks when they're still wet from being inside the egg. From what I could gather, you had to separate them so that the male chickens could be killed.

They were useless since they couldn't lay eggs. Uncle Katsuhisa said that it might seem sad to kill them, but eventually, we would learn to be kind of like farm kids—farm kids understood the meaning of death. They understood how death was part of life. When he said that, my mother and Auntie Fumi frowned at him. They did that all the time when he was talking. That meant he had to stop talking.

After they frowned, there was a silence. I looked around and saw Lynn playing with some kids closer to her age. "Come on!" she called, and I ran after them. Sometimes older kids didn't like me around, but Lynn always made them play with me. We played until bedtime, and that night Lynn and I slept on the floor in the living room. There seemed to be a million crickets singing around us. The half-moon shone through the windows. My sister and I practiced our howling and barking so we would be able to talk to our dogs if our mother ever let us get any. Our mother came into the room to quiet us down. She looked tired and worried for some reason. In fact, she looked as if she might cry. So we settled down immediately.

cynthia kadohata

Seeing my mother like that made me
remember Iowa. Here are the things I already
missed:

1. The view. When I used to look
    outside my bedroom window on
    summer mornings, I saw nothing
    but corn and blue sky. In winter I
    saw snow and blue sky.
2. The Iowa State Japanese-American
    Bowling League. Every Saturday
    all the Japanese Americans for
    many miles around met at a bowl-
    ing alley in the middle of the state.
    My father's friends always gave us
    coins and told us what songs to
    play on the jukebox.
3. Mrs. Chan, the Chinese widow
    from down the street. We'd helped
    her plant tomatoes in her yard ear-
    lier that summer. By the way, she
    was the one who could take out
    her top teeth.
4. Snow. Making angels and snow-
    men was fun. Sometimes our father
    played with us. Once, our mother

came outside, and Dad actually threw a snowball at her. I thought she would faint, but after a long pause she smiled slightly.

5. My parents. They worked regular hours in Iowa. Here in Georgia they planned to leave for work every day very early in the morning. Our father would work two jobs, and our mother would work overtime if it was available. I already missed them.

chapter 4 きらきら

OUR APARTMENT BUILDING in Chesterfield was one story, shaped like a U around a courtyard. The inside of our apartment consisted of two very small bedrooms, a living room, a kitchen, and a bathroom. The wallpaper in the kitchen was dirty and peeling. Mold grew on the wall in the bathroom. Lynn and I followed our parents from room to room.

Our mother was obviously unhappy, which made our father unhappy. She didn't complain, but we could all tell how she felt because she wore a look like she did when she had a headache. Our father said, "Kiyoko, we'll make part of the living room into your sewing area. That'll be nice." She didn't answer. He said, "There's a free refrigerator here!" She still didn't answer. He said, "I'm going to paint the girls' room white with pink trim!"

Finally, she spoke. "There's only space for two small beds and one small desk in their room. Where will we put Katie's desk when she starts school?"

"Let me think about that," he said.

"We'll have to put it in my sewing area."

Nobody answered. I felt guilty because my future desk would ruin her sewing area. I didn't even want to go to school, anyway. I forgot to think nonsense words. That's why my mother was able to read my mind and know I felt guilty. She pulled me to her and hugged me. "It's not your fault!" she said, suddenly cheerful.

A swing-set frame sat in the middle of our courtyard, but there were no swings. Some of the kids liked to climb on the frame. Everyone played outside all the time because there was nothing to do in our small apartments. When the fathers wanted to talk outside, they sat on the curb in front of Mr. Kanagawa's apartment. He was sort of their leader.

His wife, Mrs. Kanagawa, didn't work, so when fall came, she took care of the preschoolers all day. I could have gone to kindergarten, but when I went for one week, I cried and screamed so much that my parents thought maybe I shouldn't start school until first grade. There were three of us preschoolers, but the other two were younger than me, so I played by myself. I could read and write a little bit, I could color or jump rope alone, but mostly I played with Bera-Bera. He chattered on and on, even when I was trying to take my nap.

At 3:30 each afternoon, I would watch out the window until I saw Lynn walking down the street—there were no sidewalks in our small town. I would run outside to meet her. Mrs. Kanagawa said I was like Lynn's pet dog.

Most days in southern Georgia were warm and humid. After school Lynn, some of the other kids from the residence, and I used to lie about and stare at the clouds. If it was cool enough, we would play dodgeball. At night before we went in for bed, the parents would sit on the stoop and we children would either play or lie on our backs and watch the Milky Way. Watching the sky was all Lynn's idea. Just as Mr. Kanagawa was the leader of the fathers, Lynn quickly became the leader of us kids. She was a big believer in watching the sky. She pointed out that if beings from outer space ever came, they would probably want to talk to us. So we should keep our eyes open.

Some nights before bed Lynn and I would make our wishes. First we made selfish wishes, and then we finished with unselfish wishes. One night, though, Lynn said, "Let's just make selfish wishes tonight."

That seemed bad, so I said, "Okay."

"You start."

"I wish for a bed with a canopy and a box of sixteen crayons instead of eight."

"I wish that I'll go to college on a scholarship someday. I wish I'll be homecoming queen in high school. I wish we could afford a nice house."

"I wish we had a better hot-water heater so the water wasn't so cold all the time."

She didn't say anything. She probably felt bad, like me. I felt like maybe we should make some unselfish wishes.

She said, "Maybe we can each make one unselfish wish."

"I wish for a house for you and for Mom."

"I wish you would be happy forever."

That left our father. I didn't know what he wanted most. It seemed the only thing he wanted was to take care of us. Every time it was his birthday, we got him aftershave lotion that our mother paid for. He always seemed to like it.

I said, "I wish Dad never loses his hair like Grandpa did before he died."

The last thing before we went to bed, Lynn and I would talk about what we should spend our money on the next day. Every weekday our father gave us a nickel to get ourselves a treat. But that night Lynn said, "From now on we're going to save our nickels to help Mom and Dad buy our first house. That way, instead of just wishing for a house, we're helping to really get one."

That was a hard thing to agree with, but I didn't argue because Lynn was boss. Usually when Lynn got home from school, we would go to the market, where we studied the treats for a long time before picking out what we wanted: often a powdered-sugar doughnut. Then we would walk along the highway eating. It was sad to think all that was over, but I guessed a house would be worth it.

"Good night, Katie," she said.

"Good night."

During the autumn the sultry air made us tired but not too tired. If it was too hot, we took a nap before supper. Then Lynn would read to me. Since she was a genius, she could read anything, even *Encyclopædia Britannica.* We had the "P" volume from *Encyclopædia Britannica* that somebody had left behind in our house in Iowa when we moved in. We planned to read it all the way through. Our other favorite book was *Silas Marner.* We were quite capitalistic and liked the idea of Silas keeping all that gold underneath the floorboards.

Whenever Lynn was late from school, I would cry. Mrs. Kanagawa would tell my mother whenever I cried. My mother said I was a crybaby, but Lynn said I was actually happy because it was my nature to be so, just like it was Lynn's nature to be a genius. It was also Lynn's nature to be a little bossy. Mrs. Kanagawa told me that.

Lynn didn't seem to be making many friends at school. So she spent a lot of time with me. That was the way I passed the first year in Georgia: waiting all day for Lynn to come home and then playing with Lynn until bedtime. When summer came again, we played all day and all night until bed.

By the time I was six and ready to start school, my accent had already become very Southern. I no longer called my sister "Lynn," I called her "Lee-uhn." I was kind of a celebrity in my neighborhood, the little Japanese girl who said "you all" instead of "you," and "You don't sah-eee" instead of "Really?" Sometimes people would pay me a few pennies to talk to them. My sister encouraged this enterprise, and soon we were rich.

We kept the money in a moldy hole in the tile under the bathtub. Once a month we would count it.

The day before I started first grade, Lynn sat me down for a talk. She gave me talks only when something very, very serious was happening. She always told me the truth and didn't treat me like a baby. It was she and not my parents who'd first told me we were leaving Iowa.

We sat cross-legged on the floor in our room and held hands and closed our eyes while she chanted, "Mind meld, mind meld, mind meld." That was our friendship chant.

She gazed at me solemnly. "No matter what happens, someday when we're each married, we'll own houses down the block from each other. We'll live by the sea in California."

That sounded okay with me. "If y'all are going to live by the sea, I will too," I said. I had never seen the California sea, but I imagined it was very pretty. She leaned forward then, and I knew she was going to get to the point of this talk.

"Have you noticed that sometimes people

49

won't say hello to Mom when we're out shopping?"

"Uh-huh."

"Well, some of the kids at school may not say hello to you, either."

"You mean because they don't know me?"

"No, I mean because they don't want to know you."

"Why wouldn't they want to know me?" Who wouldn't want to know me? This was a new idea for me. Our father had always thought we were quite amazing, and Lynn, of course, had always thought I was perfect, so I thought of myself as rather amazing and maybe even perfect.

"Because, there's only thirty-one Japanese people in the whole town, and there's more than four thousand people in the town, and four thousand divided by thirty-one is . . . a lot more of them than of us. Do you understand?"

"No."

Lynn's face darkened. That was kind of unusual. "Haven't you noticed that Mom and Dad's only friends are Japanese?"

"I guess so."

"That's because the rest of the people are ignoring them. They think we're like door-mats—or ants or something!" Now she was really angry.

"Ants?"

She suddenly reached out and hugged me to her. "You tell me if anybody treats you like that, and I'll take care of it!"

"Okay." Sometimes Lynn didn't seem to make sense. That was because I was so young and she was such a genius.

Then she kissed my face and said, "You're the most wonderful girl in the world!"

Right then my mother came in with scissors to chop off my long straight hair. This was a ritual all the local Japanese mothers performed the day before they sent their daughters off to school for the first time. My mother cut my hair to my chin and made me sleep in pin curls all night. This was okay with me because Lynn wore curls during the school year, and so I knew it was what big girls did. But when I woke up and took out the bobby pins, I was too shocked even to cry or scream or stomp around the house. I looked like a feather duster! After the shock wore off, I was ready to cry and scream and stomp. "I'm not going to school!" I screamed. "I'm not!" I stared in the mirror, closed my eyes, and stared again. I stomped one foot and then the other. Lynn gaped at me. She looked kind of half amused and kind of half horrified.

My mother "fixed" my hair by combing it. She said I looked like Ava Gardner, who Lynn said was a beautiful famous actress with about seventy thousand boyfriends. If she was so famous, why had I never heard of her? Still, I liked the idea of looking like a movie star. I calmed down a bit. My father said, "You look like . . . you look like . . . well, you look awfully cute!" It was the middle of the night, because that's when my parents went to work. They were both running a little late so that they could spend time with me on my first day of school.

My mother put me in a yellow chiffon party dress. I liked the dress. And I was start-ing to like my hair. As a matter of fact, I started to think I looked quite ravishing. After my parents went to work, I just sat there and wouldn't move in case my hair got mussed. I wouldn't even let Lynn try to comb my hair because it was already perfect. When Mrs. Kanagawa came over to check on us, she oohed and aahed over how cute I looked.

I felt like an empress on the way to school. I wasn't even nervous as we walked on the shoulder of the road to school. Lynn was just wearing a jumper, but her hair was curled like mine. She stopped when we stood across the street from the school.

"That's it?" I said. The school wasn't any bigger than our little apartment building.

"That's it," she said.

I was a little disappointed. I didn't understand what all the commotion had been about or why I was wearing my best dress.

When we walked into the schoolyard, I saw that all the other girls were dressed more like Lynn, in jumpers or plain skirts with white blouses. Lynn walked me to my class line, where I stood on the number—Classroom #100—by myself. All around me girls were playing and talking. They all wore curls, but no one's hair was as curly as mine. Finally, the bell rang, and about a dozen kids lined up behind me.

Somebody tapped me on my shoulder, and when I turned around, the girl right in back of me said, "Are you Chinese or Japanese?"

"Japanese," I said.

Another girl called out, "What's your native name?"

I wasn't exactly sure what she meant, but I said, "Natsuko." That was my middle name. It means "summer"—when I was born. My sister's middle name was Akiko, which means "autumn"—when she was born.

Then a girl said to me, "What happened to your hair?"

I could tell she wasn't insulting me; she was just curious. I felt my face grow hot. I didn't answer.

Then the teacher came to walk us into class. She smiled at my dress and said, "Going to a party?" I would have gone home right then, but I wasn't sure I could find the way without Lynn.

When class opened, the teacher said

everyone could sit where they wanted, just for today. All the girls screamed and giggled and rushed this way and that around me. Then they all sat down. At recess I stood in the middle of the schoolyard in my party dress. Once, two girls from my class walked by not far from me, and I called out, "School sure is boring, isn't it?" but they ignored me. Lynn came out to stand with me. She said she'd stayed inside a few minutes after the bell because her teacher wanted to tell her what a good girl she was.

Later that afternoon, when I didn't know an answer, my teacher looked disappointed and said, "I've heard your sister is very smart." I didn't hold this against Lynn, though. I was proud of her.

Shortly before I'd started first grade, my mother had started to gain a lot of weight. She peed a lot, she threw up a lot, and she drank a lot of water. She ate weird things, like spoonful after spoonful of barbecue sauce. We had to keep several jars of barbecue sauce in the cabinet. My sister sat me down, and after our mind meld she told me that we were going to have a baby brother.

My mother gave birth to Samson Ichiro Takeshima while I was in first grade. His middle name means "first son." All the nurses at the hospital took turns coming to see him when he was born—they had never seen a Japanese baby before. Sam was covered with bruiselike marks on his backside, the way Japanese babies sometimes are. Nobody had hit him, that's just the way their bodies are. It was funny how so many people ignored my mother, but they were all fascinated by this little Japanese baby. Then, when he grew up, they would probably ignore him and treat him like an ant! I liked to watch the nurses leaning in toward the glass, cooing over little Samson. I was proud of him because I thought he was the cutest baby in the world.

Not long after my mother brought him home from the hospital, she returned to work at the factory. She was assigned a late shift at that time and never finished working until mid-evening. Mrs. Kanagawa took care of Sam during the day while Lynn and I were at summer school. Lynn wanted to go to summer school so one day she could graduate high school early. I had to go to summer school because my parents made me. After school we would run feverishly home to take care of our new brother.

At night Lynn, Sam, and I would lie outside in the empty street and watch the stars. Sam would lie in the middle as Lynn and I chanted, *"Kira-kira, kira-kira."*

One hot night our father was staying overnight at the hatchery, which he did sometimes to save driving time and get more sleep. Our mother was already in bed. We snuck outside in our pajamas and lay in the middle of the street. I liked wearing my pajamas outside. Someday when I was a grown-up lazy person, I would wear my pajamas whenever I wanted. I liked to ask Lynn questions, because she knew so many answers.

I said, "What would it feel like if all the stars were made of bits of ice and they fell from the sky and landed on us?"

And Lynn said it would feel nice. How did she know that? Because she knew everything!

I asked her, "What would happen if all the tea in China suddenly fell from the sky and landed on us?"

She said that would feel nice too.

Finally, we got sleepy and went inside. Our bedroom now contained two beds and a crib. When Lynn needed to study, she used the kitchen table. Some nights I liked to put Sam on my little bed so he could sleep with me instead of alone. I did not want the *oni*—ogres who I knew guarded the gates of hell—to take my brother in the night. I hugged him to me all night. When he was one year old, I remembered something: At some point since he had been born, I had lost Bera-Bera and never even noticed.

chapter 5

きらきら

SAMMY WAS THE calmest baby in the world. He hardly ever cried. Lynn took care of me, and I took care of Sammy. And we all took care of one another. It's hard to believe that for the next couple of years nothing happened. It was wonderful. We spent all our spare time with one another. In my sister's diary entries from those years she chronicled what days Sammy learned how to walk and talk, what our homework assignments were every night, what time our parents got home from work, and any other details she could think of. She had the neatest handwriting in the world. Sometimes I would watch her write in her diary, and I was amazed at how perfect her writing was.

Occasionally, my uncle brought us on camping trips. Lynn said that his camping trips were the most fun thing she ever did. I agreed with her about that. She asked me, "Do you agree with me all the time just because I say so or because you really, truly agree with me?" I didn't see the difference between the two things, so I just said I didn't know.

Sometimes, in case she became a famous writer, Lynn practiced writing little stories in her diary:

Once upon a time a funny witch cast a spell on all the world's creatures. Suddenly, all the animals that used to be able to fly could only walk and all the animals that used to walk could now fly. So you saw horses soaring through the sky and preening on rooftops; you saw birds by the thousands running through the streets and along high-

*ways. And the fish, don't even
mention the fish! The fish learned
to drive and the humans lived in
the sea. The End.*

I think the whole reason she wrote that
story was that she loved the idea of living in
the sea. That was one thing that never varied
about Lynn: her love of the sea. Living by the
sea in California was what she looked forward
to second most in life, after going to college.
Owning our own home was third for her, and
first for our mother.

Every week that passed was nearly the
same. School was boring and homework was
boring. Playing with my brother and sister was
fun. That's the way the days went, with no
surprises.

Everything started to change the winter
I was ten and a half. One unusually warm day
in January all the kids from the apartments
were playing dodgeball after school. Lynn was
in charge, as always. She said, "Katie, you
stand there. Toshi, you stand here." And so on.
She chose a little boy to stand in the middle.

The boy flung the ball at Lynn. That wasn't very smart, because Lynn was quick. But the ball flew up and hit her chest. She staggered back. Everyone except me laughed. My sister got almost cross-eyed, and everybody laughed more. I didn't laugh because I knew Lynnie better than anyone.

"Lee-uhn!" I said. I ran over to her.

She swayed a bit but said, "I'm fine."

"What happened?"

"I don't know. It seemed swirly for a second."

"What seemed swirly?"

"Everything."

I followed her inside. She went right to bed and slept through dinner.

She wasn't able to help me with my homework that night. That worried her. I got straight C's at school. So far I had never gotten a B or a D in any subject. My father said that "C" stood for "consistency" and that he was very proud of me, so long as I was doing my best. I guess that in terms of grades I was just as consistent as Lynn was, which, when you thought about it, was surely something to be proud of. Lynn got straight A's. She loved school.

The next day, however, she didn't even go to school. Even when she was sick, she usually begged our mother to let her go to school. This was the first time I'd ever seen her happy to stay home. When I got home, a doctor was just leaving. Mrs. Kanagawa was there. She said the doctor had put Lynn on iron pills.

At dinner that night my father said he thought maybe Lynn just took after our mother, who also used to get tired a lot. In fact, my mother said that once when she was a child, she had spent almost the whole year in bed from fatigue, and nobody knew why. So I figured Lynn was just going through a phase, the same as my mother had.

One night, though, she woke up crying. I couldn't remember Lynn crying since the day we left Iowa. When she woke up, she said she'd dreamed that she was swimming happily in the ocean.

She sobbed. "The sun was shining. Everything was beautiful."

"Why did that dream make you cry?"

"Because it was only my spirit swimming in the ocean, and not really me."

"What's a spirit?"

"It's the invisible part of me."

I didn't understand her reasoning at all. First of all, I didn't understand what she meant by "invisible part of me." Second of all, her dream sounded happy to me. But I also knew that Lynn was always right, so I was a little worried. Suddenly, she said, "Don't worry, sweetie, I'm okay. Go to bed."

So I went to bed.

The next day was Saturday. She lay in bed all day. She didn't want to be bothered or talked to or anything.

I said, "Do you all want me to go get you some candy?"

She said, "No."

I said, "Do you all want an apple?"

She said, "No."

I said, "Do you all want some company?"

And she said, "No."

Even with her occasional fatigue, Lynn still managed to help me a lot. The truth was, without Lynn, I probably would have gotten some D's. I didn't understand the point of school. You sat in a chair all day and read words and added numbers and followed directions. You weren't allowed to chew gum. You weren't allowed to write notes—not that I had anybody to write notes to. But, still. And you weren't allowed to talk unless you knew the answers to the teacher's questions.

Lynn actually liked reading stories and adding numbers. And she actually knew the answers to the teacher's questions. She was fourteen. She had gotten so pretty that the other girls had to take notice of her, if only to be jealous. Of course, Lynn had always been very pretty. Her skin and eyes were radiant, and her hair was strong and shiny. Even though all the other girls curled their hair, she had started to wear hers straight and so long that it touched the middle of her butt. Gregg, the most popular boy in her class, liked her. Finally, one of the popular girls, Amber, broke ranks and became Lynn's first best friend. That is, I felt I was still Lynn's best friend, but Amber was maybe her second best friend. Amber becoming Lynn's second best friend was the other big event that winter.

It did get to be a little annoying. Amber came with us everywhere. She was one of those really girlie girls who paint their fingernails and even their toenails. She said she was going to be a model someday, and she walked very upright. All winter and spring she and Lynn walked back and forth in the living room with books on their heads. Amber said, "This is the way models walk."

I said, "Seems pretty ridiculous to me!" I looked to Lynn for agreement, but she frowned at me.

Amber had brown hair, which she said she was going to dye blond when she turned sixteen. She had brown eyes instead of blue, which was a tremendous disappointment to her. She stuck out her pinkie when she held a cup. And, worst of all, she was making Lynn weird. For instance, Lynn had started to wear lipstick when our parents weren't around.

Many days Lynn tried to get me to spend time with her and Amber as they walked in the living room with books on their heads, told secrets while sticking out their pinkies, or giggled in front of the mirror while experimenting with makeup. Amber hated camping, so now Lynn didn't want to go camping. The thing was, I still loved camping. I think Lynn's feelings were a little hurt that I didn't agree with her about camping anymore. I felt strange not agreeing with her.

One day when we were eating roast chicken, I ripped the thigh from the drumstick with my hands. Our parents were at work. Sammy followed my example and ripped a chicken leg in two.

I said, "Let's see who can put the most food in their mouth at once!" Sammy and I filled our mouths.

Lynn said, "Katie, that's not very ladylike."

I couldn't answer because my mouth was full. Sammy and I thought that was pretty funny. When I'd finally swallowed everything, Lynn looked worried. She wiped food from my chin and said firmly, "Katie, you know you're not going to be able to act like that much longer."

She brought her plate to the sink and left the room. I knew that Lynn was actually trying to help me. Usually when she was trying to help me, I didn't mind. In fact, usually I was eager to please her. But this time I didn't speak to her all the rest of that night. That was the first time I ever shunned her for a whole night. I was waiting for her to apologize, but she never did because she didn't even notice I was shunning her. The next day she wanted me to practice walking across the room with her and Amber, but after awhile I was bored and said so. This hurt her feelings, which made me feel bad.

One weekend it turned out that Gregg and another cute boy from Lynn and Amber's class were going to be going camping near the same place where Uncle Katsuhisa used to take us. Lynn and Amber begged Uncle to take us camping that weekend, and he agreed. The thought of Amber going camping was a bizarre thought indeed. It was hard to picture her sitting around a campfire with a book on her head. She and Lynn wanted the whole family to go camping, for authenticity. That is, they wanted the boys to believe that the whole family just happened to be going camping at the same time and in the same place as the boys just happened to be going camping.

My parents had started to work more and more. They used to go camping sometimes, but they never thought about having fun anymore. My father was exhausted from working ninety hours a week. My mother was exhausted from working overtime whenever she could. So they didn't go camping with us that weekend for Lynn and Amber's Great Boy Hunt.

Uncle, however, brought his whole family, even my Auntie Fumi, who hated camping. She had grown chubbier, and she didn't like the outdoors, maybe because it might muss her beehive hairdo. The whole time we drove, she stared worriedly at the sky, even though there were only a few white clouds.

We parked the truck near the campgrounds and hiked about a mile. Auntie Fumi looked worried the whole time. She kept staring into the forest, as if she thought a tree might fall on her. But she never complained—it wasn't her nature. For a while as we walked I tried to talk to Lynn and Amber, but they were obsessed with a cute dress they had seen in a store. Instead, I walked hand in hand with Sammy or pushed his stroller over the bumpy ground. *He* thought Amber was stupid too.

When we found our campsite, my cousins David and Daniel and I helped Uncle pitch the tents. Then he put us in charge of starting a fire. He went into the tent with Auntie. David said they were trying to make another baby. He said they did it all the time. I wasn't quite sure what he meant. But years ago when our parents were trying to make Sammy, Lynnie had told me never to go in our parents' bedroom without knocking. She didn't tell me not to listen at the door, however, so I knew trying to make a baby was hard work that required a lot of effort and grunting.

I turned my attention to starting the fire. It took me several minutes to keep the match from blowing out in the wind, and then the match almost burned me, so I flung it away. I guess when I flung it, it landed on a sleeping bag, because the next thing I knew, David was shouting, "Fire!" David was a devil like me, at least that's what Uncle liked to say. David seemed excited about the fire. He helped me throw all of our drinking water, as well as all of our sodas, on the sleeping bag, which sizzled and smoked. Finally, when it was charred but wet, we tried to hide it behind a tent since we didn't want Uncle to see it. Then we set our minds to starting a fire again. But in a moment Daniel pointed at the tent, and we saw smoke snaking from the back.

When we ran behind the tent, smoke billowed into our faces. We tossed mounds of dirt on that weird sleeping bag. Amber and Lynn sat behind the tent, probably telling secrets. They watched the whole event with mild disdain, but I thought I saw a certain yearning in Lynn's eyes, as if maybe she would rather be setting fire to sleeping bags than sticking her pinkie out and telling secrets.

When Uncle and Auntie finally emerged from the tent, Uncle sniffed the air and frowned. Smoke coiled through the air. David and I tried to look innocent. Uncle stamped on the dirt over the sleeping bag until finally the smoke stopped. He started to get annoyed, but then Auntie said to him, "They're just children."

Uncle needed to walk back to the truck

and drive into town to get us water, sodas, and a sleeping bag. To his credit, he only yelled at us for a short time about burning the sleeping bag. When he got back from town, he started the fire, which seemed to cheer him up. Then he announced that he was going to shoot us some rabbits for dinner with a bow and arrow. David, Daniel, and I begged to come. Uncle said we could all watch from a distance if we wanted. He said he could shoot a rabbit from thirty yards. Auntie (holding Sammy), my cousins, and I followed Uncle, with Lynn and Amber following us. They walked arm in arm and whispered the whole time.

We came upon an opening. Uncle Katsuhisa suddenly knelt and moved stealthily forward. Auntie's eyes glowed with pride. He put up his palm to still us, and we stopped. He'd apparently sighted a rabbit that I could not see anywhere. I surprised everyone, including myself, by shouting out, "But Bera-Bera is half rabbit!"

That disturbed Uncle's concentration. He turned to me and opened his mouth, but Auntie spoke first. "She'll be quiet next time." She pulled me to her. I was embarrassed by my outburst. Lynnie and Amber would think I was being a baby if I was worried about a stuffed animal. I didn't even know where Bera-Bera was anymore.

I could feel Uncle Katsuhisa move into another zone, he and the bow becoming one. I felt queasy. We walked awhile more, and then he let loose of the arrow, and it screamed forward, piercing its mark cleanly. For the first time I saw the rabbit, still and bloody. That was the last thing I remembered. The next thing I knew, the faces of Lynn, Auntie, the twins, and Sammy were looming over me as I lay on my back. I sat up and saw Uncle holding three rabbits. Their ears were exactly as long as the ears of Bera-Bera. The trees started to spin as I looked at the bloody rabbits. Someone said, "There she goes again!"

chapter 6 きらきら

WHEN I OPENED my eyes once more, Amber was squealing and giggling. Two lanky boys were joking with her. One of them had red hair and about a million freckles. The other had hair as yellow as a dandelion. Amber was practically slobbering over them. Lynn leaned over me. "I know where Bera-Bera is," she said. "He's safe in the closet."

I didn't like how Lynn still thought of me as a little kid. I sat up. "I'm okay."

Lynn knelt beside me. "You don't have to say that, you know. There's nothing wrong with loving a stuffed animal."

"I'm *fine*." But Lynn looked really worried. Even though she was friends with Amber, she still worried about me all the time. But lately, she worried about me the way I worried about Sam, the way you might worry about a baby or young child. I stood up. "I'm fine."

One of the boys glanced at Uncle and said, "That was really something, sir." He turned to Amber. "Can *you* shoot an arrow, Amber?"

He was just making conversation, even I could see that. But Amber got flustered and said, "I could certainly try." She looked at Uncle Katsuhisa.

"It's not a toy, Amber."

Auntie Fumi touched his arm. "She seems very mature," said Auntie Fumi. I heard her whisper, "She's a guest."

He relented, showing Amber how to concentrate, aim, pull, and shoot. She glanced at the boys, who gazed admiringly at her. That seemed to give her confidence. She stepped away from Uncle, aiming at nothing that I could see. She stuck her pinkies out. Just as she let go of the arrow she tripped, and the arrow whizzed through the air about a foot from Uncle's head and pierced a lollygagging bird before sailing to the ground twenty feet away. David jumped up and down. "My turn! My turn!" he said.

We followed Uncle as he walked to the bird. We all stood around while he touched his head in wonder. "That could be my head," he finally said. "That could be my brains."

"I'm sorry," said Amber, which didn't seem quite enough.

For some reason the boys seemed pretty impressed with Amber's display. They invited Lynn and Amber to eat dinner at their campfire. Lynn asked me if I wanted to come, but I said no. My sister and her silly friend left. I immediately felt lonely.

David, Sammy, and I buried the bird and headed quietly back to camp to eat rabbit. The rabbit tasted kind of like chicken, except more like . . . rabbit. I didn't like it much but didn't say so. David said that if you ate too much rabbit, your ears would grow longer and fur would grow on your butt where a tail might be. Sammy didn't seem to notice anything special about it.

Uncle was a good talker, and Auntie was a

good listener. So as we sat around the campfire later Uncle talked while Auntie nodded as if he were telling fascinating stories. Sometimes I wondered what Lynnie and Amber were doing. Actually, Lynnie didn't like me to call her "Lynnie" anymore, but I did anyway. She thought "Lynn" was more grown up.

I tried to concentrate on what Uncle was saying. The thing is, Uncle's stories never seemed to come to a point. For instance, that night he told us about the time he and his first wife *almost* saw a legendary tornado. But they didn't actually see it. They just happened to pass through a town the day before a tornado came through and ripped the town to shreds. The interesting part of this story to me was that he mentioned his first wife. My parents spoke only in hushed tones of Uncle's first wife. Apparently, Uncle had loved this woman very much, but in a different way than he loved Auntie. I didn't know what the difference was, but I knew that Auntie knew. I could tell by the way she grew irate whenever this ex-wife was mentioned. But she never said anything about it.

Then Uncle spent about twenty minutes telling us about the time when he was young and he and a friend decided to practice target shooting with some cans. They didn't hit anything, even after they moved to two feet away. Again, that didn't seem like much of a story to me, but Auntie laughed appreciatively as Uncle described missing the cans, and missing them, and missing them again.

Then he told us about the time a friend of his found a bag containing twenty thousand dollars. The owner of the bag claimed the money before the friend could "make off." Now, the interesting thing about this story to me was that Uncle seemed a little disappointed that his friend hadn't "made off." Uncle was a very honest man and would never steal anything himself, but he seemed to admire people who did. He kept a lot of books at his house about famous criminals from history.

Most of the story about the twenty thousand dollars consisted of Uncle coming up with ideas about how his friend could have ended up with this money, how he could have spent the money, and how Uncle himself would have spent this money had he been the one to find it. In this last version of the story no one ever claimed the money, so Uncle wasn't stealing anything. Even in his imagination, it was impossible for him to steal anything or do anything really bad. I guess that was one reason why Auntie loved him so much.

Uncle kept talking. The fire warmed my face. I wondered where Lynn and Amber were. When Lynn first became friends with Amber, she told me a lot of stuff, including that some girls did something called French kissing with boys—something to do with tongues. It sounded a little complicated to kiss with your lips *and* your tongue. I was not good at doing two things at once. I wondered whether Lynn might now be French kissing with these cute boys. Someday when I was older, I might try French kissing, but only with my true love, Joe-John Abondondalarama. One reason I didn't do so well in school was because many times I was up half the night enjoying my active dream life with Joe-John Abondondalarama. He would have two first names because his father was named Joe and his grandfather was named

John, so his parents decided on Joe-John. We would get married, and I would be Katie Natsuko Takeshima Abondondalarama. Here is our story:

We would meet at the Grand Canyon when I was seventeen. I would be gazing at the awe-inspiring chasm when a freak gust of wind would lift me up and fling me over the rail. I would hang in the wind over the Grand Canyon, moments from certain death. My life would flash before me. I would regret so many things. I would wish I hadn't talked back so much to my parents. I would wish I had kept my part of the bedroom cleaner. I would wish I could have gotten at least one A in school. My screams would pierce the air. And suddenly, a strong arm would reach out and catch me. At the end of this strong arm would be Joe-John Abondondalarama. The sun would glisten off his black hair. His eyes would shine like the sun. Thunder would sound in my heart! Lightning! Eventually, we would have seven children.

Even Lynn did not know about Joe-John, although someday she would be my maid of honor.

Once in awhile I preferred to tell myself alternate versions of how I would meet Joe-John. For instance, I was working on a new story in my head. It was called "The Bathroom Story." It went like this:

Joe-John and I would be at a birthday party. We would never have met. Somehow or other (I was still figuring out the details), we would both end up in the bathroom together. Maybe I was admiring the shower curtain, and he came in because he spotted me from behind and liked my sweater. The door accidentally locked behind him, and we couldn't get out. The party was so noisy that no one could hear us shouting. The window was stuck. We were in a back bathroom that rarely got used. Time passed. We talked until midnight, and then we had no choice but to sleep in the bathtub together. All night we would tell each other secrets, and then by morning we would be in love. As I said, I was still working on the details, but that's the gist.

That night, when my sister and Amber returned, they set their sleeping bags next to each other and lay whispering away from the rest of us. Then Lynn remembered me and called out, "Katie, come bring your sleeping bag!" I thought about shunning her for temporarily forgetting about me, but what good would that do? I dragged my sleeping bag over, and they started to tell me about their evening: how Lynn had kissed Gregg, and how Amber had almost kissed the other boy, and how they were the cutest boys in the class. Even Amber acted as if I were her good friend. Then Amber asked me whether I liked any special boys at school. At that moment I felt very close to my sister, and even to Amber. And how I loved camping! Moss hung off the tall pines around us, and the full moon shone through the moss. I remembered how all during my childhood, whenever the moon was full, Lynn used to sing me the "Rabbit on the Moon" song:

Usagi Usagi nani mite haneru
Jugoya otsuki-san mite haneru

I told Lynn and Amber my Joe-John stories. I was pretty pleased about my future with him. Lynn and Amber laughed and laughed at me! They didn't even pretend not to laugh! They didn't even laugh really, they kind of honked and tried to get their breath. They became so hysterical, they seemed to be in danger of choking. Frankly, I thought all that honking sounded pretty unladylike, but I was too nice to say so.

When they finished laughing, I realized they weren't laughing *at* me—they thought they were laughing *with* me. They had thought I was just joking about Joe-John Abondondalarama. Lynn hugged me and exclaimed, "I love you, Katie!"

Amber said, "You're great! You're the funniest person I ever met!"

What could I say? I basked in their praise. I felt pretty phony pretending I'd just been kidding, though. I wished I had my own friend.

chapter 7 きらきら

MY FATHER'S HOURS changed sometimes. His newest schedule was to work for ten to twelve hours, then eat and sleep a few hours at the hatchery, and then get up and work six hours. When he wasn't working at his main hatchery, he worked at a different one in another town. My mother's current shift ran from 4:30 A.M. to 1:30 P.M., plus three hours of overtime.

When school let out for the summer, Lynn spent the first week at Amber's house. Mrs. Kanagawa couldn't watch Sam and me that week because she was tending to her sick mother in Oregon. Since I was almost eleven, I felt I was old enough to take care of Sammy and myself all day. But my mother didn't think so. She decided that Sam and I would have to go with her to work every day. We could sleep in the car until her shift ended.

The poultry processing plant where she worked was in the next town, about an hour from our house. The same man who owned the hatchery for egg-layers where my father mainly worked also owned several processing plants for his roasters and fryers. His name was Mr. Lyndon, and he was the richest man in the county and one of the richest men in Georgia. I'd never seen him, but my father had seen his car once—a Cadillac—and a girl at school said she once saw him from behind. He never came to his processing plants or the hatchery. If there was a problem that needed his attention, he sent an assistant. He was an invisible legend in the county: the big, mean, rich Mr. Lyndon. His great-great-grandfather, his great-grandfather, his grandfather, and his father had all lived in Georgia.

I thought of him as my mother drove up in the darkness to the processing plant. His wife was supposed to be very beautiful, with finger-nails one inch long. Once when President Eisenhower had visited Georgia years earlier, he supposedly ate dinner at the Lyndons' home. Their home was a former plantation mansion. He had torn down the old slave quarters on his property. In its place his wife had hired gardeners to create an azalea garden that was supposed to be gorgeous. Her garden was supposed to be so big, you could get lost in it. Such a world as they lived in was difficult to imagine. Someday when we owned a house, I would get my mother an azalea plant so she could start her own garden.

Previously, my mother used to have to drive my father to his job and then drive her-self back to the plant. But now we owned a new car. That is, it was an old car, but it was new to us. Rust was eating away at its paint, but my mother said that in its heyday it had been lovely. She had bought the cheapest car she could find. She didn't want anything to take away from the house she longed to buy.

I got to sit in front, which was a treat and made me feel like a grown-up. My brother slept in back. I'd sat in front only once before in the truck with Uncle Katsuhisa. You could see everything in the world out the front windshield.

The road was empty, like so many roads we had driven on in my life. The highways in southern Georgia were famous for how dark they were, no light anywhere—no farm lights or streetlights or town lights. We passed a swamp, and I locked the door. The biggest swamp in Georgia was across the state. It was called Okefenokee Swamp, which means "Land of Trembling Earth" in Seminole. Our local swamp was called Brenda Swamp, named after a girl who died there way back before I was born. Her ghost lived in the swamp. It was looking for her parents. I stared out into the darkness, saw the moss hang like drool from the pines. When the wind blew, the swamp did seem to tremble.

How I would hate to wander in that murky water for the rest of eternity looking for my parents! I looked over at my mother, but she was lost in thought. I looked back at my brother, who was sleeping peacefully. I looked back out at the swamp and thought of Brenda. She was ten when she died. I thought I saw something move out there, but then I didn't see it anymore.

I tried to stay awake to enjoy the ride in the front seat, but I fell asleep, and when I awoke, we were slowing down and I saw the first light I'd seen in awhile. Four tall lampposts stood near the fence surrounding the plant. Insects were like death to a poultry plant, so the lights were allowed to shine on the building but no lights could be attached to it. Inside, my mother said, everything was made of aluminum and steel. There was no wood, even in the chairs and tables in the reception office. Wood attracted insects. There was no vegetation inside the fence.

Poultry was one of the biggest industries supporting the economy of Georgia, but that didn't stop many people who did *not* work with poultry from looking down on those who *did*. That and the fact that I was Japanese were the two reasons the girls at school ignored me.

Sometimes when Mom and I ran into the girls from my school with their mothers, the other mothers would not even acknowledge mine. My mother did not have to work. My father would have been happy to support all of us; in fact, I think he would have preferred it. But there was the important matter of the house that we needed to buy.

Even within the plant, there was some snobbism. When we first moved here, my mother had started out working in the so-called dirty areas of the plant. That was where the blood and guts and feathers and such were handled. The workers from the clean sections weren't allowed in the dirty sections, and the workers from the dirty sections weren't allowed in the clean sections. The dirty-section workers were the lowest of the low.

The previous year my mother had been promoted into a clean section, where she worked cutting drumsticks and thighs off the bodies of the chickens. She was good with her hands and she wore gloves while she worked, but even so, little cuts often marred her delicate hands. And her wrists were so sore some days, she could hardly move them after work.

She drove into a dirt parking lot outside the fenced area and parked near the few trees. There were already hundreds of cars parked. I looked around. It was so terribly dark. She looked at me. "Keep the doors locked," she said. "I'll come out on my break."

"Okay." I gazed across the parking lot to the dark highway. "Why can't we sleep inside while y'all are working?"

"You might steal a chicken."

I knew she didn't mean me in particular, but anyone. There were two things the factory manager possessed a morbid fear of: insects and stolen chickens. Where I might hide this stolen chicken was another matter.

My mother looked at her watch. "I'm late for my shower. Stay in the car unless absolutely necessary." There weren't quite enough showers for all the employees at once, so everyone was assigned a shower time. My mother got out and hurried toward the plant.

I locked the doors and climbed in back to

be near my brother. I laid his head in my lap. When he was sleeping, he was like a rag doll. Nothing could wake him. I ran my hand over his head. I liked to feel his new bristly crew cut. A long truck moved through the gate at the fence. I could hear the clucking and squawking of chickens. The truck moved behind the building. I couldn't see, but I knew the chickens were being unloaded.

A big man walked slowly around the building. He didn't see me. Maybe he was checking for people stealing chickens.

Another car drove into the lot and parked near me. A woman about my mother's age and a girl about my age got out. The girl glanced at me, hesitated, and then walked over. I lowered my window. Her mother glanced over but kept heading toward the plant.

"Hi," said the girl.

"Hi."

"What're you doing?"

"Waiting for my mother. What're you all doing?"

"I do the laundry every morning. Then my uncle comes and picks me up on his way to work, and I hang around his office." She paused, then repeated proudly, "My uncle works in an office."

"What kind of office?"

"Insurance." She spoke casually but was obviously very proud. I wished my father worked in an office! "I do the load for the shift that gets off at four thirty in the morning. Then my uncle brings me back during his lunchtime and I do one more load, and then my mother takes me home. I'm saving for a new school dress."

"Can I come in and see the plant?" I said.

"You might steal a chicken!" she said, as if scolding me. I saw the man walking around the building again. She saw me studying him and said, "That's the thug."

"What's a thug?"

She looked at him. He was watching us now, but then he kept walking. She leaned toward the car. "Didn't your mother tell you? The workers are trying to unionize. The thug works for Mr. Lyndon. He discourages union activity. He doesn't let any of the employees gather in the parking lot, even if they're not talking about the union." She checked her watch and said, "Gotta get the first load going!"

She ran to the building and disappeared around a corner. Insects clustered around the lights at the fence. I wished we would get a house soon so my mother could stop working here. After a pause I decided that I wished that the girl I'd just met would get a house too, and maybe a new dress. My leg was falling asleep, so I shifted Sammy's head in my lap. He looked so cute. I rolled up the window so the thug couldn't get in and harm him.

When I next woke, the hot sun was slanting through the windshield. I saw that Sam was still asleep. We used to joke that if nobody remembered to wake him, he would just sleep through the day and night and not get up again until we called him for breakfast. Lynn was like that too. That girl could sleep. Sometimes she slept for twelve hours in a row. But me, I slept restlessly a lot, and sometimes it seemed I barely slept at all. It was funny, because even though I was bad a lot, I also worried a lot about how bad I was. When I worried, I couldn't sleep.

Perspiration spotted Sam's forehead. I

wiped him off with my shirtsleeve. I opened a window, and a muggy gust of air shot across my face. If I'd known how to drive and had the keys, I would have driven the car into better shade. Then I saw my mother rushing across the asphalt surrounding the plant. She seemed even smaller than usual as she hurried over. Lynn was already a few inches taller than our mother. I pushed the car door open.

"I was so worried!" she said.

"I saw the thug walking!" I said.

"What thug?"

"The man who works for Mr. Lyndon to keep anyone from gathering and doing union activity."

"Who have you been talking to?"

"A girl. I kept the door locked!"

"You are not to talk to that girl again. And you are not to call that man a thug. He is an employee of Mr. Lyndon. Do you understand me?"

"Yeah—yes. But, Mom? What's 'union activity'?"

"A union is when all the workers get together and fight the very people who have provided them with a job and the very people who pay the employees money to give them the means to buy a house someday."

"So a union is bad?"

"It's wrong to fight the people who are trying to help you."

She looked at Sam sleeping so peacefully. I felt proud of myself that we were doing fine. She noticed the sweat on Sam's face and got in and started the car. She pulled directly under a tree but kept the motor running. She tried the air conditioner. Sometimes it worked and sometimes it didn't. This time it worked. The noise was loud, though. Once, we had turned on the air conditioner and driven through various neighborhoods where my mother could admire the houses. Now she lay back against the car seat. I noticed a few white hairs that I'd never seen before. She was thirty-three, two years younger than my father. She was starting to look tired all the time. Usually when my parents were home, they were eating or sleeping. They didn't eat with us because we ate earlier. We never did anything together anymore.

After a moment I heard my mother breathing evenly. Many minutes passed, and I worried she was going to be late. I didn't know what time it was, but she must have been on her lunch break. Still, I didn't think she got long for lunch. I watched the shadows of the trees move over the dirt. Finally, I said, "Mom?"

She shot up as if I'd thrown ice on her. She didn't even say good-bye, just mumbled something about showering and then sped back toward the factory. I had never seen her run so fast before. Her feet pounded across the asphalt. Because she'd come out here into the dirty world, maybe she needed to take another shower before she started work again. I felt guilty that I hadn't woken her sooner.

When Sam finally woke up, I fed him rice balls and water. We played with special little kid cards for a while. To tell the truth, he was so young, it was kind of dull to play cards with him. I let him win two games to make him happy, but I took seven games, just so he wouldn't forget I was the older sister.

Later I read some books to him, and afterward we slept some more. When our mother drove us home, we were tired from doing nothing all day in the hot car. My mother smelled funny. The factory workers weren't allowed to take unscheduled breaks, so they all wore pads in case they needed to use the bathroom. It smelled like my mother had used her pad. I decided that someday when I was rich, I was going to buy the factory and let the workers use the bathroom whenever they wanted.

chapter 8 きらきら

WHEN WE RETURNED home from the factory, we were surprised to find Lynnie lying in bed. She didn't feel well, so Amber's mother had sent her home. Her temperature was normal, but she looked kind of green.

"She looks gross," I said.

"Shut up!" snapped my mother. I stepped back, as if she'd struck me. I had never heard my delicate, polite mother say "shut up."

"It came on suddenly," Lynn said. "We were eating cookies and talking about school in the kitchen, and all of a sudden, I got sick."

"Is Amber sick too?" asked my mother.

"She feels fine. But I feel dizzy when I sit up." My mother turned to where Sammy and I were standing.

"You two sleep in the living room tonight. Maybe it's contagious." I drew Sam a step back. My mother seemed to be searching her mind. "Maybe it's the measle? You never had it. Katie either." My mother spoke perfect English, but every so often when she was upset, she slipped. She didn't seem upset on the outside, but I knew she was inside. It was like the time she broke her leg and she kept saying, "I breaked my leg." I drew Sam another step back.

Lynn got tired more often lately. My parents talked about her a lot. Meanwhile, they scolded me, and even Sammy, more and more often. Our parents didn't really have time for us anymore because they liked to spend all their extra energy thinking about Lynn.

When Lynn felt good, she had a lot of energy, so I never thought of her as sickly. She was the only one of us who ever went to the doctor. The doctor usually gave her suckers,

cynthia kadohata

which made Sam and me jealous. Also, she got to stay home from school whenever she was sick. So I had thought of her as lucky. But today she seemed worse than usual.

My mother made me take Sam a couple of doors down to watch TV at the Muramotos' apartment. They were the only ones in the apartments with a TV. Television was such a treat. Fortunately, the Muramotos liked *The Twilight Zone,* so we got to watch that every week with them. Now we let ourselves in and sat on the couch with Mrs. Muramoto, who was watching the news. She loved the news because her husband had a low, clear voice, and she said that if he were *hakujin*—white—he could work as a newsman on TV. He wasn't home now. He was working with my father at the hatchery. Sometimes I thought he made his voice sound lower than it was naturally. He liked to sit alone in the kitchen reading the newspaper out loud as if he were a newsman.

"Where's Lynn?" asked Mrs. Muramoto. She was a quiet woman who worked for a tailor.

"She's tired again," I said. I always told people she was "tired," not "sick." We watched the news and a couple of game shows, and then I took Sammy back home. My parents were in the bedroom with Lynn, so I filled the bath for Sam and read to him while he sat in the bathtub. That was his favorite thing: getting read to in the bathtub. After his bath I got his pajamas for him and made up the couch for him to sleep on. Ordinarily, I didn't like to do work around the house, but taking care of Sam was the exception.

Unfortunately, if Sam was sleeping on the couch, that would leave the living-room floor for me. I didn't see why we couldn't sleep in our regular beds. If Lynn was contagious, we would get sick just from living in the same apartment. Her germs were probably all over the place by now.

I took a bath in Sam's old water and laid out some blankets on the living-room floor. When I was a little girl, sleeping on the floor always seemed like a treat. We used to beg our mother to let us sleep on the floor. It was like camping. Now that I was older, the floor felt hard. In a few minutes my mother came in looking annoyed. I knew it was because I hadn't wiped the ring around the bathtub, but I didn't say anything. I was in a bad mood because the floor was hard.

My mother seemed exasperated. She was kind of crazy about cleanliness. "How many times do I have to tell you?" she said. My father came up behind her. Even he seemed annoyed with me, and he almost never got annoyed.

"Katie," he said, "how many times does your mother have to tell you to wipe the ring in the bathtub?"

"I don't see why I have to sleep on the floor," I said.

My father's face darkened. I felt a little scared. He never got truly mad at us, ever. That was our mother's job.

My mother looked as if she was going to cry. But I was famous for being hardheaded. Maybe it was because Lynn had always let me have my way. So now I pulled the covers over my head. I was shocked when my mother pulled the covers off and yanked me up by my arm. My father rested his hand on her to restrain her. She started crying. I didn't know what was going on: It was just a bathtub ring. My father looked at me sternly. "I want you to clean the bathtub *now*," he said very quietly.

I walked into the bathroom and shut the door behind me. I sat on the floor for a few minutes to think, but I was getting sleepy, so I cleaned the bathtub. I had to admit it took only a couple of minutes. When I got out, my parents were in their bedroom. I could hear them talking but couldn't hear what they were saying.

I stopped at my bedroom and put my ear to the door. All was quiet. I looked around to make sure my parents were still in their room. Then I opened the door. The light was on, and Lynn was staring into space. She didn't even seem to notice when I opened the door.

"Lynnie?" I said. She turned to look at me, her face blank. "Y'all need anything?"

"Like what?"

"I dunno. Food?"

She shook her head. "You're not supposed to be here. I could be contagious."

"What's wrong with you?"

"I don't know. Anemia, I guess. That means I need more iron and have to eat liver. I have to

103

stay in bed all day tomorrow. You and Sam have to go with Mom again."

"We could stay with you."

"Dad says no, you might get sick."

"Anemia is contagious?"

"No, but maybe I have something else."

"Like what?"

"The doctor doesn't know."

Sometimes when I was younger and I got sick, my parents wouldn't let Lynn in the room with me. But she used to sneak in anyway, so she could take care of me. She used to worry about me quite a bit. Now I went into the living room and lay on the floor next to the couch. I got up and checked to see if my brother's forehead felt either too hot or too cold. He felt perfectly normal.

By the time I woke up, my father had already left for work. It was still dark. My mother woke Sam and me and told me to dress my brother. She said our auntie Fumi, who didn't work, was going to drive out and spend the day with Lynn. It must have been serious if Lynn couldn't even take care of herself.

Sam was half asleep as I dressed him. He whined a bit: "Why do I have to go? It's hot in the car."

"I know. Go get your toothbrush for later." He hurried away—he always listened to me.

I grabbed the lunches our mother had made for us. We followed her out of the house and got quietly in the car. I decided to sit in back. I didn't feel like being grown-up today. As we drove along the dark highway Sam leaned against me as he slept. We passed the swamp, and I watched for Brenda, the little girl who had died. I also watched for swamp lights, the weird lights that locals were always saying they saw in the swamps.

Sometimes I thought I saw something moving through the trees. But then I would realize that I had just seen moss swaying in the wind. Then I really thought I saw her! She was a pale girl running in a white dress with a dog at her side. I lowered the window. The humid air rushed in. Brenda wove through the trees before moving deeper into the swamp, so I could no longer see her. I turned to check whether my mother had seen, but she was staring straight ahead.

My mother hadn't said a word since we'd left home. I could tell that she was worried about Lynn. And even though I couldn't see him, I knew that my father, probably hard at work right now, was worried too. The measles did not seem like such a horrible thing. I'd known many children who had gotten the measles. From what I'd heard, anemia was not so terrible either. Auntie Fumi had been anemic once. And yet my parents were very worried. I decided that was because they loved us so much, even though we weren't always good. Lynn was better behaved than I was, of course, and so was Sam. But even if I got sick, I knew my parents would be very worried about me.

I was sleepy, but at the plant I tried to stay awake so that I could watch out for the thug. My mother hadn't said anything else about him. She hurried inside for her shower. A short time later the laundry girl's mother parked across the lot. I remembered that my mother had said not to talk to the girl. But she waved at me, so I had to wave back. Then she walked over, so I had to lower the window. She peered into the car at Sam. "I have a brother too, but he's older," she said.

I had to talk to her now, because it would have been rude not to. "His name is Sam. I'm Katie Takeshima."

"I'm Silly Kilgore."

"What kind of name is Silly?"

"It's short for Sylvia." Silly was pale, with kind of messy pale hair and pale eyes. Very skinny, like me.

"Oh. My name is short for Katarina." Actually, it was short for Katherine. I wasn't exactly precisely telling a lie, because even though my birth certificate said Katherine, Lynn had always told me that my real name was Katarina.

"Are you going to come here every day?"

"Just for a week. Then I have to go to summer school because my grades aren't so good. I'm going to go to Africa and study animals when I get big."

"I'm going to be a doctor."

"Can girls be doctors?"

"I can."

"Really?" I paused. That was news to me. I had never seen a girl doctor. I looked around. "Where's the thug?"

"They had some trouble at the other plant. He had to go there." She added proudly, "My mother backs having a union."

I didn't answer.

"I'd better get to work," Silly said. She ran off.

I slept for a while, woke up and fed Sammy a little rice, slept awhile more, and then woke up for good as the sun rose over the fields. I decided to walk through the gate and explore the plant.

The plant was a long rectangular building with a few windows high up the walls. On one side of the plant a garbage can lay in the dirt. I set it up and climbed on it. If I stood on my tippytoes, I could just see into one of the narrow windows. Everyone inside was dressed in white. At first I couldn't pick out my mother, but then I saw her small back. She was the tiniest worker in the factory. She expertly sliced a couple of legs off the body of a chicken. Then she sliced the drumsticks from the thighs and sent the drumsticks down one conveyor belt and the thighs down another. At the exact moment that she finished, another chicken arrived and she cut the legs off it. Over and over. I couldn't see her face, but the faces of the workers I could see were blank, perfectly so. Most of the workers were women.

I could just make out a sign titled THE THREE RULES OF MEAT PROCESSING. Underneath the title it said: 1. HYGIENE. 2. HYGIENE. 3. HYGIENE. My mother sometimes said proudly that this plant was the cleanest in Georgia. Some of the poultry plants were supposed to be filthy. She said that the chickens at this plant were special gourmet chickens that Mr. Lyndon's wife served guests at the mansion. We'd never eaten any of these special gourmet chickens. Every Christmas there was a lottery and an employee won two chickens. But my mother had never won.

I heard a cracking sound, and the next thing I knew, the corroded metal of the garbage can began to collapse and I fell to the ground. I lay on the ground for a moment, the way my father had taught me to do when I fell. "Make sure you're not hurt before you move," he had told me. When I sat up, I saw my legs were bloody. The thug was standing over me frowning. He had permanent frown lines between his eyes, and he was taller even than my father.

He looked behind me, and I saw another man approach. I felt sick to my stomach.

Then Silly ran up. It was a regular convention! "Hi, Uncle Barry," she said to the man who'd just arrived. Her uncle looked down on me and helped me up. He was wearing a real button-up shirt, and he held himself with a kind of pride.

"Are you okay?" asked Silly's uncle Barry.

The thug said, "What's going on here?"

"They're just little girls, Dick."

Dick scratched at a bite on his cheek. "Well, get them out of here."

Barry took our hands and led us away from the plant.

Silly said, "This is my new friend Katie."

He stopped and shook my hand, just as if I

were a grown-up. "Nice to meet you, Katie."

His button-up shirt made me feel I should be very polite. "Nice to meet you, sir."

Then he let go of my hand, and he and Silly got into his car. I watched them drive off. Her uncle's car was pretty nice. It looked like it was only a couple of years old.

Back in my mother's car Sam shunned me for a few minutes because I had left him alone. But he never stayed mad for long. He was little Mr. Sunshine. That was why I loved him so much. Dick the thug had paused by the building, watching me. I locked the doors.

Over the next few days Silly tried to work as fast as she could so she had time to come out and talk to me. We shared our rice balls and seaweed with her, and she shared sandwiches with me and Sam. The bread on the sandwiches was kind of amazing. You could tear out the white middle section and press it into a hard ball of dough before you ate it. Or you could twirl it into long strings and wrap it around your tongue. Sammy had never seen bread before. He loved it.

It turned out that Silly's father had died shortly after she was born. Her uncle—her father's brother—was like a father to her. Her uncle had owned a sign store once, but it had gone out of business. Silly needed to work to help pay for her school clothes. In her spare time she also helped her mother fold union flyers.

She made me feel lazy. I did manage to clean up after myself a little, but other than that I didn't do much of anything except take care of Sammy. The area around my bed was the messiest part of the room, except for the area under my bed, which was even worse. Every time it was my turn to do the dishes, I always had an excuse—or else, if Lynn felt well, I let her do them for me. And yet my parents could afford to buy me my school clothes.

Silly and I exchanged phone numbers. I promised her she could use Lynn's bicycle and we would go riding. She was the only kid I knew who did not even own a bicycle!

chapter 9

LYNN GOT BETTER and didn't get sick again for so long that I figured everything was fine. My parents still kept a careful watch on her, but even they seemed more relaxed. On my eleventh birthday I got to invite Silly over. I was so excited, I didn't even mind that my mother let Lynn invite Amber over for *my* birthday. I baked a cake, which was lopsided but tasty, and Silly and I spent the whole day calling ourselves the Shirondas and singing and dancing wildly to the radio. We made up special dance steps and pretended we were on *The Ed Sullivan Show*. Amber acted like we were stupid. She tried to get Lynn to think we were stupid too. But Lynn thought we were "too cute for words." That was her new phrase for me. She and Amber walked around with their heads held high. They didn't even need books on their heads anymore. They just naturally walked like that! Amber was mad because she wanted to go down to the schoolyard in case any cute boys were hanging about. But my mother said Lynn had to stay home because it was my birthday.

So they just sat in the living room and held their heads high while Silly and I danced. Then Silly and I told ghost stories. Then we dressed up Sam in funny clothes until my mother scolded us. Finally, we went outside to wait for Silly's mother to pick her up. I walked to the street with her to help her carry her water jugs. She lived in an area just outside of town where many people did not have running water, so whenever she came over, she filled big jugs to take home. I asked my mother to come outside so she could bring a jug too. She frowned but agreed. I knew she'd frowned because water didn't grow on trees.

We sat on the front stoop. Across the street some grown-ups sat talking and laughing. Some kids from another apartment played kickball in the street.

Silly's mother, Mrs. Kilgore, drove up and got out of her car. She and my mother nodded politely at each other and tried to think of something to say. Mrs. Kilgore was a no-nonsense woman. She didn't believe in small talk. She looked at my mother and said, "There's a union meeting next Wednesday at the church on Frame Street."

"Yes," said my mother coolly. My mother was scared the union supporters would get them all fired, even her. She wanted a house, and she didn't care if she couldn't use the bathroom during work or if her fingers were so stiff that she couldn't move them when she got home. If that's what a house cost, she would pay the price.

"The meeting's at seven thirty in the evening," said Mrs. Kilgore.

"Wednesday evening is bad for me," said my mother.

They left then. "Mom, why is Wednesday bad for you?"

"That woman makes too much trouble." My mother pulled me down on the stoop beside her. I thought she was going to tell me Silly couldn't be my friend anymore, but instead, she took my face in her hands and frowned. "Did you want to grow your hair long again?" she said. I'd expected her to say something more serious, but I didn't know what.

For a while she'd given my hair a permanent every few months, but something about the permanent solution made my hair fall out. So now I was back to pin curls every night. "I hate pin curls!" I said. She didn't answer. The day was fading into evening. There were no streetlights, but the street was lit by the lights from the apartments and from a motel down the way, the sign flashing on and off, on and off. M-O-T-E-L, in aqua neon.

"Your summer school teacher said you got a good score on your achievement test."

"Yeah." She frowned, and I said, "I mean, yes."

"Nobody understands why you don't get better grades."

"I'm trying."

"Your father is very disappointed." That surprised me. I didn't think my father was ever disappointed in me. She patted my knee and stood up. She had always seemed younger than the other mothers, partly because of her size, but also because her face possessed a childlike quality. But tonight she grunted when she stood up. And even in the dim light, her face seemed older than it had even the previous month. I remembered the white hairs I'd seen. She opened the door and I followed her in.

That night I tried to concentrate on my homework for Monday, but it was boring. We had to read a story about a man who discovered a secret treasure. He bought lots of nice clothes and ate fancy dinners, but he lost his most valued friends because he grew obsessed with his money. We were supposed to write three paragraphs answering the questions:

117

What is the author trying to say by describing the expensive dinners in such detail? What is the theme of the story? How did the main character change at the end? It was a good story, and I liked it. But I didn't know how to answer those questions.

Amber left, and Lynn, who had read the story, took the time to tell me the story was about greed. So I wrote that the theme of the story was greed. And then I couldn't think of anything else to write. Finally, I wrote, *The descriptions of the dinners really describe greed. Greed is bad. People shouldn't be greedy. At the end of the book the main character isn't greedy anymore.* I added a few other brilliant remarks. And then I folded the paper in half and put it in my book. I would probably get another C, which was good enough for me.

That night Sam fell asleep before me, as always. He shouted out in his dream, "Call me *Mister* Takeshima!" I laughed and got up and kissed him and made sure the sheet was snug around him.

"Good night, Mister Takeshima."

I turned around and was surprised to see

Lynn sitting on the floor next to the couch. She was clutching her knees to her chest.

"Gregg is moving away," she said.

"I thought he was coming over for dinner one day."

"He was, but then he found out he was moving. They're already packed up. I haven't told anyone else."

"Not even Amber?"

"Nope."

"Are you in love with him?"

She thought this over. "No. I guess I like him, but I don't love him."

That was good. In my most humble opinion, Gregg was a little pukey. His hair looked like something you would brush a horse with. And when he talked, little bits of saliva collected at the corners of his mouth. He was certainly nothing like Joe-John Abondondalarama. Of course, I didn't mention this to Lynn.

Lynn returned to the bedroom. We used to wake each other up sometimes in the middle of the night and say what was on our minds. But Lynn hadn't done that in a long time. Usually when she used to wake me up, she had wanted to talk about college. I had secretly decided not to go to college, but I thought that maybe I would move to the same town as her. Then we could share an apartment in a tall building, the way she'd always dreamed.

Lynn had seemed sad about Gregg.

I got up and went to the bedroom and sat by her bed. "Lee-uhn?"

"Uh-huh."

"There's another boy in your class I think is cuter."

"Who?"

"I think his name is Clifton."

"Clifton! Oooh! I thought you were serious." She laughed. "You're so funny!"

That made me realize I must have said something stupid. "Well, he's okay," I said defensively. That was the way it was lately. Whenever I tried to talk to her, she made me feel immature, even if she didn't mean to. I went back to the living room and fell asleep.

The next day Lynn felt so tired, she didn't want to get out of bed. I cooked her an extra helping of liver and told her to chew well.

Chewing well was what my mother always told me to do when I was sick. It was a Sunday. Lynn slept most of the day. By evening, when I tried to feed her, the food just fell out of her mouth. She didn't have the energy to chew. I even offered to chew it for her, but she said, "Gross."

My mother decided to take her to the hospital. My father was at work and nobody in the building was home because it was bowling night, so my mother called Uncle Katsuhisa to come take care of Sammy and me. Uncle didn't like to bowl because he only liked games where you had to think. I watched as my mother put Lynn's jacket over her pajamas. Lynn staggered out the door.

I locked the front door and waited for my uncle to arrive. Sammy's forehead was all wrinkled. He was calm, like my father, so it was unusual to see his forehead wrinkled that way. My mother always liked to say he was never going to get wrinkles because he hardly ever frowned. But now he was probably worried about Lynnie.

When Uncle Katsuhisa knocked on the

door, I made him give me a password. He said with irritation, "Open up now, young lady, or bear my wrath." That happened to be the password, so I opened the door.

Uncle came in with Auntie Fumi and David and Daniel. They did everything together. Unlike my father, Uncle worked only one job, and Auntie didn't work at all. David and Daniel probably got to see their parents all the time.

I didn't know what to expect from Uncle and Auntie. Last time I had seen them, they had been fighting. They were like that. One day they were madly in love, and the next day they were fighting. And then the next day they were madly in love again.

Usually Uncle Katsuhisa was boisterous, but today when he came over, he was restrained. Plus, Uncle and Auntie were snapping at each other a bit. Obviously, they'd been fighting.

He said, "One thing I can't stand is a woman who spends money unnecessarily."

She said, "A woman needs a coat."

He said, "In ninety-degree weather?"

She said, "It won't always be ninety."

And so on. Then they stopped, and we all just sat there glumly.

All of a sudden, Uncle Katsuhisa stood up and announced, "We are going to play Scrabble!" He said that as if playing Scrabble were as fun as going bike riding or something.

I wasn't a good Scrabble player, but it was better than sitting around the living room staring at one another. I set up the game. Uncle sat in a chair and said, "It's family time!" Sam could already read simple words, but he was too young to play. He sat beside me. Uncle looked suspiciously at him, as if he might somehow help me cheat. David and Daniel studied their letters. I was first. I studied my letters. There didn't seem to be a word in them. Uncle cleared his throat. After a moment I could hear his foot, first *tap, tap, tap,* and then *whompwhompwhomp* on the floor. I sensed I was already ruining our family time. He peeked at my letters and threw his hands into the air.

"Think, Katie. Think, Katie. *Think*, Katie!" He looked at me as if I were possibly brain damaged. I'd seen him look at Auntie like that sometimes. He never actually called anyone stupid, but sometimes he looked at them as if he thought they were. "We're waiting, Katie," he said. "Take your time."

"I can't see anything I can do." It was hard to think with all that whomping.

"Take your time."

"Katsu, leave her alone. She's thinking," said Auntie Fumi.

"I'm trying to help," he said defensively. Then he looked at me as if it were my fault Auntie had scolded him. He looked at her. "Can I just say one more thing to her?"

"No," she said.

He peeked at my letters again and shook his head.

"You have to rise to the occasion," he said to me, sneaking a look at my aunt. She frowned.

I still didn't see what I could do. Scrabble was not my specialty. Now that I think of it, I suppose I didn't have a specialty. I looked at my letters: "S-Z-O-G-V-W-Q." Then I saw it, or thought I did. I put down "S-O-G." I happily picked up three more letters—all vowels.

I smiled up at my uncle. He was staring at the board. Then he leaned over, his head in his hands. He didn't speak for a long time. He groaned loudly over and over.

"Isn't that a bit melodramatic, Katsu?" Aunt Fumi asked.

"Isn't that a word?" I finally said.

"No, that is not a word," Uncle said. "That is not a word. That is *not* a word." He hadn't lifted his head. He hit his forehead on the table a couple of times. He lifted his head. "What do they teach them in school today? She's thirteen years old."

"She's eleven."

"Thirteen or eleven, that is still not a word."

My aunt stroked my face lovingly. "That was a good try, dear."

"'Soggy' is a word," I said. "Like 'foggy' and 'fog'?"

"Fumi, just tell me one thing: Is she doing this to torment me? I don't know if she's doing this just to torment me. If she's not, okay, but if she is . . ."

My aunt looked at me gently. "Honey, look

at those letters you put down. There's a word right in those letters." She stroked my face. "What other word can you spell?"

I looked at Sam. He was mouthing something. It looked like "Oh." He did it again: "Oh."

"Oh," I murmured.

"Ssss," said Sam. I picked up the "G" and returned it to my slate of letters, leaving "S" and "O."

My uncle stared at my word "so." He turned to Sammy. "*Thank* you, Sammy."

"Sometimes it's hard to see the obvious," Auntie said sweetly.

David looked sideways at his father, who glared at me again before turning his glare to the board. David, who was always my pal, ceremoniously plucked a few letters from his collection and then set down his letters and spelled "S-P-E-R-M."

Nobody spoke. Actually, I wasn't certain what "sperm" meant. But I could guess.

Uncle Katsuhisa just stared at the board for a moment. He nodded a few times.

"Where did you learn that word?" said Auntie Fumi.

"From Dad."

Uncle Katsuhisa didn't speak, but he turned red. He said, "It's a legal word, that's the important thing for our purposes."

Auntie glared at him. The phone rang, and she went to get it. Nobody moved while she talked. When she was finished talking, she walked back into the living room and just stood there. Then she burst into tears and ran out of the room. We all stared after her. Uncle got up slowly and left the room. In a moment we heard him and Auntie talking.

Then it got very quiet in the other room. I cleaned up the Scrabble game. David, Daniel, Sammy, and I just sat around doing nothing, which was about as boring as it sounds. Finally, David and I snuck into the hallway to peek at what Uncle and Auntie were doing. They were in the kitchen, and the radio was playing softly. They were holding each other very tightly. They weren't dancing exactly, but just stepping back and forth in time to the music. I could tell it made David happy to see them like that, even though it embarrassed him because it was kind of goofy.

I had to interrupt their dancing to ask, "Auntie, was that my parents?"

She and my uncle stopped dancing. "Yes, it was your mother," she said. "She told me to tell you . . . to tell you that everything is okay. Don't worry, sweetheart. She told me to tell you that."

chapter 10

きらきら

W~HEN~ L~YNN~ ~RETURNED~ from the hospital a couple of days later, my mother insisted that she was basically fine. Apparently, Lynn's anemia was "acting up" and she just needed more liver.

Every day I sat by her bed and fed her rice and liver. I always saved a little liver for Sam, so he wouldn't get anemic too. Then, after I fed Lynn, I would give her her iron pills. When she was being obstinate, I had to force the pills down her throat and hold her mouth closed until she swallowed. Once she tried to bite me.

Sam and I were supposed to sleep in the

living room until Lynn got better. My parents had bought me a little cot. I worried that Lynn was lonely by herself in the bedroom, but when I peeked into her diary, I read this:

> I feel bad that the kids have to sleep in the living room, but it's really nice to have my own bed-room. I like the privacy a lot.

I didn't think of myself as one of "the kids." But I guess that was how Lynn still thought of me.

After I fed Lynn, I got my pajamas from the closet, said good night, and left the room. Later that night I opened my eyes and saw her sitting on the floor next to my cot.

"What is it?" I said.

"Amber dropped me."

"Dropped you, like as a friend?"

"Uh-huh. I don't really care. She was phony."

I could have told Lynn that a long time ago! For a moment I got a funny feeling that I was the older sister and Lynn was just a little girl.

Lynn stood up. "Well, good night," she said.

"Good night."

She didn't move; she just stood there. The motel light from down the street cast a vague flashing shadow on her face. I could see she had been crying.

"Good night," she said again.

"Good night!"

The next day after summer school I ran into Amber walking with her friends. Lynn was sick in bed that day. Amber said to me, "*What* is that you're wearing?"

I was wearing a polka-dot dress Mrs. Muramoto had made for me. As usual, I thought I was quite a fashion plate! But these girls started laughing at me. They were all wearing pedal pushers.

"You're a phony!" I said.

"You're a heathen!" she said.

I didn't know what a heathen was, but I said, "You're a heathen too!"

"Then you admit you're a heathen!" she said.

I thought about Lynn lying sick in bed and pushed Amber's shoulder. She pushed me back. I balled my right hand in a fist and punched her. She moved her face, so I barely hit her. She didn't seem hurt at all, but I thought for a moment I had broken my hand. What a hard face that mean girl had! Then a passerby rushed over and made us all go home.

That night I felt an incredible anger toward those girls. I thought I hated them. I had never hated anyone before. It felt awful.

I told my parents that Amber had dropped Lynn. I wished I hadn't, because I saw how it hurt them. Then I was glad I had, because after I told them, they talked for a long time in the kitchen, and afterward they announced that we were going to the bank to take out a loan.

"I thought you didn't want to borrow money from the bank!" I said.

"We want to get your sister's house," said my mother.

That night Lynn was more cheerful than she'd been in a long time. Awhile ago we'd stopped hiding our money in the bathroom. Now we hid it in the closet. Every so often we counted the change out and placed it in paper rolls Lynn picked up from the bank. Then every few months Lynn would go to the bank to exchange the rolls for bills. Sometimes I went with her. I didn't like the bank. I didn't see why a bunch of strangers got to keep everybody's money in vaults. If a robber came to our apartment, I would hit him over the head with a lamp. So I didn't need a bank, personally.

We had saved a hundred dollars. Sammy still got treats because he was just a little boy, but Lynn and I hadn't bought candy in a long time.

The night before we went to the bank with our parents to apply for a loan, Lynnie, Sammy, and I handed them a pink envelope with our money in it. Our note just said, *From Lynn, Katie, and Sam.* We had put Sammy's name on it too because we were a threesome.

When our parents saw all the money we had saved, our mother started to cry and hugged Lynn and then started to sob and said over and over, "I love you so much, Lynn." She sobbed so hard, she ran from the kitchen, and in a moment we heard her bedroom door slam. Our father kissed us all and then went into the bedroom to talk to our mother. The money was supposed to make them happy, so we felt a little weird.

Lynn felt good enough to wash dishes while Sammy and I tried to do headstands against the refrigerator.

The next day when I got home from school, I stayed in my school clothes and accompanied our parents, Lynn, and Sam to the bank. Sam was wearing a button-up shirt that was a little small for him. Lynn felt good again that day. We pulled a bunch of chairs around the loan officer's desk and sat mesmerized as he asked our parents for some papers that they'd already filled out. As he looked them over sometimes he frowned and sometimes he nodded with satisfaction. I counted seven nods of satisfaction and only three frowns. He stood up to shake hands with my parents. "We'll be in touch," he said.

Two weeks later the bank approved the loan, and the very same day we took Lynn out to look at houses. She found one the first day. She picked out a sky blue one, because she said that when I was a little girl, I had told her I wanted our first house to be sky blue. We moved in not long after.

It was a small house, a lot like our apartment except for two extra rooms: a small dining room and a small alcove off the living room. There was even the same small motel not far away, its sign blinking all night. We just lived on the other side of the motel now. But it felt far away from our old apartment.

The first things out of our uncle's truck were our desks. Lynn and I were going to put our desks in the alcove. Our father and uncle walked into the empty house carrying Lynn's desk.

"Where should we put it?" said our father.

Lynn looked at me. "Which side do you want?"

"You choose first."

We both knew which was the good side: the side facing the big magnolia in the next yard.

"You can choose," said Lynn.

"Anytime, girls," said Uncle Katsuhisa.

"I'll take that side," I said, pointing to the bad side.

"You're just saying that," said Lynn.

"I don't mind standing here all day, girls," said Uncle. He was pretty tired, since he and my father had just finished loading all the stuff into the truck a few minutes earlier. He and my father set down the desk, and Uncle said we'd flip a coin.

He threw a quarter into the air, somehow caught it behind his back, and slapped it on his forearm. Lynn and I looked at each other.

"Tails," said Lynn.

Uncle glanced at the quarter and quickly put it into his pocket. He said, "Lynn's got tails, and it was heads."

I said, "I'll take the side that faces toward our old apartment. That way, I can see where we used to live."

So Lynnie got first choice even if she didn't want it.

She was radiant as she watched our father and uncle carry boxes into our new house. Actually, I thought of it as Lynnie's house. I held Sammy while she stood in the living room excitedly watching all the commotion. Lynnie loved commotion.

My father and uncle had painted the week

before, so as we lay in our bedroom that night we could smell the paint. I took in big breaths so I would never forget how fun it was to live in our own new house and sleep in our own newly painted bedroom with my sister and brother.

I'd heard our mother tell our father that this was just a "beginner house" and that someday we would own a "better" house in a "better" neighborhood, but I could not imagine a better house than this one. We had a grass yard in front and in back, and at night raccoons, possums, and skunks walked through the backyard just as if they lived there.

My sister got better every day, and I heard my mother telling my father that she thought the house itself was making Lynn better. I agreed. It was as if the house were healing Lynn. That made me love the house even more than I would have anyway.

A few days later Lynn, Sammy, and I planned a picnic to celebrate how good she felt. We hadn't gone on a picnic since she'd first made friends with Amber. My parents were a little worried about her going out, but they were also excited that she felt so well. It was as if she'd never been sick.

On the day of the picnic she shook me awake at dawn. "Dad left a whole dollar!" she said. I opened my eyes. Dad had told us he would leave us money to get food for our picnic.

"Shall we buy doughnuts, then?" I said.

"Maybe we want doughnuts. Maybe not."

"I wish the store had the kind with jelly inside."

"I wish that too!" She was excited. She used to love picnics before Amber came along. "I can't decide. We might want Popsicles."

Pleasure flushed my face. I hadn't thought of Popsicles! It felt nice to think about treats again, after all that time saving for a house.

Sam said, "I've wet the bed." That brought us back down to earth. I had to clean up after Sam while Lynn made us breakfast: what we called brown eggs, made by scrambling eggs with *shoyu* and sugar. It was my favorite breakfast.

After we ate, we made rice balls to take with us. We talked it over and decided to use

138

part of our money for root beer and the rest for doughnuts.

We rode our bicycles—Sam rode with me on mine. It was a lovely late-summer day. I loved the days at the end of summer. Each day before the regular school year started became more and more precious.

The wind blew hard. Decaying magnolia petals drifted on the streets as we rode. We headed south toward Mr. Lyndon's mansion—white with white pillars. We liked to see his house. My father always said it was his dream house. It was even in a book at the library, about Georgia mansions from the pre–Civil War days. When Lynn and I were rich, we would make Mr. Lyndon an offer he couldn't refuse and buy that house for my father. That would be one of the seven houses we'd get our parents. Over the years we'd gone for a couple of picnics on Mr. Lyndon's sprawling unfenced property. His property was kind of a local tourist attraction—he'd even offered tours at one time.

Lynn called back from her bicycle, "Mr. Lyndon inherited everything he owns!" I knew that, of course, because the grown-ups always mentioned it. I think they wanted to remind themselves that he had never earned his way like they did.

We stopped at the edge of one of his fields and left our bicycles in the grass.

Grass and trees stretched before us. I looked doubtfully at Lynn. Would she get tired? But she was jubilant with energy. It seemed we walked forever, but Lynn's enthusiasm never flagged. Every so often I studied Sam for signs of fatigue. But all I saw was satisfaction. Other times Sam glanced at me, to make sure everything was okay. Each time he glanced at me, I smiled furtively at him. It was our secret that I was his special favorite.

A field is a magical place. I could imagine what the past held: cows grazing, a Civil War battle, maybe dinosaurs. The tall grass tended toward blue green and waved in the wind the way I imagined weeds would wave in the sea. I loved that beautiful blue-green color.

After awhile there was nothing behind us and nothing before us except more field and a grove of trees. Lynn stopped.

"Here's the spot," she announced.

We spread out the blanket and lay on our stomachs, with our heads near the edge so we could look into the grass. I said, "We're on a raft in the middle of the sea!" Sam looked a bit apprehensive; Lynn ignored me. She drew an imaginary square as she bit into a rice ball.

"Let's see how much we can see in the square. I'll go first. I see an ant."

"I see grass," I said.

"That's what I was going to say," said Sam. He sighed. I could tell he was getting tired of being the young one and losing every game except when we felt sorry for him and let him win.

"I see that tiny piece of quartz."

"Snail poop," I said.

"Liar," she said. "I see a caterpillar! I just noticed!"

And so on, square after square, until Lynn yawned and I knew the game was over. Sam sat a few yards away eating rice and dough-nuts. What a beautiful day! What a perfect time for a nap. I lay on my back and closed my eyes. The wind tickled my face. I dreamed I was a mermaid, the fastest mermaid in the ocean. I was at the Mermaid Olympics. Thousands of fish-people watched at the Undersea Olympic Stadium. They were cheering. But in the midst of all the cheering someone was scream-ing. I had to swim to help. A little boy . . .

Lynn was already plowing toward a grove of trees. Sam shouted over and over, "Waaaaaaaa! Waaaaaaaa!" in a voice that I didn't recognize at first as his. But even before I recognized it, it was pulling me toward it. I wished I didn't run faster than Lynn, so I wouldn't have to arrive first. But since she'd become a teenager, her legs had grown long and gawky. I passed her and ran toward the screaming.

Someone had set a trap in the field, the metal kind that bites an animal until the animal is forced to chew off its own leg. The teeth dug through Sam's skin, making a circle of red on his thin ankle. For some reason his face was red, as if someone were squeezing his neck. He looked at me pleadingly. "Help me," he said. For a second I thought his foot was cut off.

I felt dizzy and started to say, "I don't know

what to do." But instead, I knelt down to remove the trap. I couldn't pull the teeth apart. I wished I could just run away and let Lynn take care of it. Then I saw how to open it: by pushing down the tabs on the sides of the trap. I pushed them as hard as I could. "Move your foot; I can't hold it!" I cried out. Sammy pulled his foot out, and I let go of the trap, which snapped shut. My brother stared at his leg and let out a wail.

"We're going to take you to the doctor," I said. "He'll sew you up and make you better."

"Sew me up with a needle?" He wailed even more.

Lynn arrived, and I felt relieved that I was no longer in charge. I carried Sam piggyback to the blanket while Lynn directed me. "Watch out, that part's hilly." Or, "Careful, you're shaking him." It seemed to take forever, and I got exhausted. We decided to use the blanket as a gurney and head back home. Lynn took the back end. I was glad she was in back because I didn't want to look at my brother's ankle. It made me dizzy. I walked backward but kept my head turned so I could see where

I was going. After just a minute I could hear Lynn panting.

We walked forever, and when we had walked forever, we did not seem to have gotten anywhere. Lynn needed to stop to adjust her grip more and more frequently, and finally, the blanket slipped out of her hands. My brother grunted as he fell. I turned to look, first at him with his shocked expression, and then at her with her expression of exhaustion.

"Can you keep going?" I said.

"Yes." Lynn picked up the blanket and we continued. But in a few steps the blanket slipped again. Sam no longer cried tears, and he no longer wailed loudly. His face was still red, but it looked almost frozen, as if he were paralyzed.

Lynn and I stared at him. His ankle had swollen like a balloon. We dripped sweat.

"I'm cold," said Sam.

Lynn looked at me. "Go get help. I'll wait with him," she said.

I hesitated. I hated being alone. I loved having a brother and sister. I did not even like walking alone half a block from the house to the mailbox. When my parents asked me to mail something, I always took Sam with me.

"You have to," said Lynn. She sat down next to Sam and stroked his face. Her own face was starting to get that green look, and she was panting, but not just from fatigue. It was also as if she couldn't breathe.

"Keep him warm, then."

Lynn nodded. Sam stared at me. "Help me," he said again.

I ran off through the field, hoping I wouldn't get lost. But after awhile I couldn't figure out which way I was supposed to go. It seemed to my memory that at first we'd walked north to get to the picnic site, and then we'd turned west. That meant that I should walk east and then south. But when I walked east, it seemed to me that I was going in the wrong direction. So then I looked around and tried to remember where the sun had been when we'd first entered the field earlier. I decided the sun had been before us: east. So we'd walked east first and then south? I checked to see where the sun was starting its midday descent. Then I realized it didn't matter which way I went. I just *ran*.

I ended up not where we'd come from, but in an unfamiliar neighborhood that nevertheless seemed familiar because it looked so much like a neighborhood I knew my mother would want to live in. The houses were "better," though not by a lot.

All the houses were almost the same. The same old frame houses, mostly white, but a few in blue, pink, or yellow; the same gravel driveways; and even the same rich man's mansion in the distance. I was on the back side of the mansion, though. Before, we had seen it from the front. I guess that meant we'd been going west earlier. Or . . . I wasn't sure. Directions were not my specialty.

I ran down the block, to the house that looked most like one my mother would have wanted, if we could have afforded it. I knocked so firmly on the door that I was surprised at the loud noise I made. Sunflowers decorated the curtains, and a plastic sunflower was stuck into the front lawn. A young white woman answered the door and was unabashedly surprised to see me.

"My goodness," she said.

"My brother! An accident! He got his foot caught in a trap." I burst into tears.

"My goodness," she said again. She thought a moment. "I think Hank Garvin is home." She turned toward the inside of her house. "Casey, stay put, do you *hear* me!"

I followed her to a nearby house, where she didn't knock, but rather stuck her head in an open window and called out. "Hank Garvin, are you home?"

In a moment a couple of men walked into the living room as the woman and I peeked in. One of the men leered at the woman while the other man came forward. She spoke to the one who came forward, but not until she had cast a disdainful glance toward the other.

"This little girl's brother has got caught in a trap." She turned to me. "Was it on Mr. Lyndon's property?" I pointed, and she nodded. "Uh-huh, Mr. Lyndon. That idiotic son of a bitch. I hate him *and* his wife."

"Show me where," said Hank. He opened the door and strode to his truck. He stopped once to see if I was following. "Come *on*."

As we got in the other man was walking

onto the front porch. I heard him saying, "Ginger, honey, you sure are looking good," but we were out of range then, and I couldn't hear her reply.

I turned to Hank and momentarily forgot why I was there. He did not look like Joe-John Abondondalarama, but he was just as handsome. He smiled at me.

"Don't worry. I got caught in a trap once when I was a kid. How old is your brother?"

"Five." Then I remembered that he was four. I blushed.

"That's how old I was. And later I ran track in high school." He smiled again. "I wasn't any good, but I made the team."

I glanced out the window, then said shyly, "Really?"

"You caught me in a lie," he said. He grinned. "It was junior varsity. Hang on!"

The truck screeched through the street and made a sharp turn. We reached the field I had just come from and jumped over the curb and onto the grass. I bounced up and hit the ceiling of the car. My teeth clattered together when I landed. For a moment I feared I'd made a big mistake by finding this crazy-driving Hank Garvin. But he was so calm, it made me calmer.

I said, "I think you go left here!"

"Here?" he said.

"Yes!"

"Hang on!"

He turned hard left while I hung on. I had never been alone like this with a grown-up white person. But I wasn't scared exactly. I felt breathless and excited. He bumped along as if he drove over fields like this every day.

"Your daddy work in the hatchery?"

"Yes. My mother works in the big plant."

"Really? My wife is helping to unionize that plant."

Lately, my mother and father sometimes talked in low voices about the attempts to unionize the plant. I'd overheard my mother say you couldn't trust anyone anymore. And Silly had told me that one of the pro-union workers had got beaten up one night. Now I felt scared. What if Hank Garvin was secretly a thug? I wasn't even sure what a thug was exactly, which was all the more reason to be scared. A thug could be anyone, anywhere.

Hank seemed to sense my fear. He drove with his knees maneuvering the steering wheel while he searched his pockets and came up with a piece of striped gum that he threw to me. He took the wheel with his hands again. I was holding on for my very life. He smiled. He was so awfully handsome. "I've never been in an accident in thirty years."

Thirty years! He was way too old for me! I put some gum into my mouth. "You go right here!" I said. "At least, I think so."

"What's your name?"

"Katie!"

"Hang on, Katie!" He veered right.

I hung on tight, and then I saw my sister and brother.

chapter 11

きらきら

LYNNIE AND EVEN Sam were both a little surprised to see Hank: He was that handsome. It was as if he had stepped out of a comic book. I felt rather important, since I had sort of discovered him. He picked up Sam and strode quickly to the truck.

"You girls sit in back!"

I thought I heard dogs baying in the distance, and I remembered I'd heard rumors about Mr. Lyndon owning vicious dogs. Lynn and I climbed in. Right before Hank started the truck, he leaned out the window and looked at us. He said, "Hang on!"

We grabbed some straps attached to the inside of the truck bed. I could see inside the cab. Sam lay wide-eyed across the seat. His eyes locked on mine. I smiled slightly and laid my hand on the glass. He smiled very slightly at me and reached his hand up toward mine. We bumped across the field again.

This time we sped in a different direction. We reached the street in a short time. Hank drove expertly but very fast. I looked behind us and saw our bicycles lying in the grass.

It felt strange to be speeding through the streets of this neighborhood where I didn't belong, in a truck where I didn't belong, with my brother hurt and my sister sick. I thought of all those stories I had to read for school and the questions the teachers always asked. What is the theme? What does the story mean? Why did the characters act in a certain way? We whizzed by the pretty houses. It seemed that at this moment I was inside a story. This was the story of my life, and I did not know what any of it meant. Despite all that was terrible about that day, I found myself exhilarated by our speed, by the sheer adventure of the moment, and most of all by the fact that, by myself, I had found this man Hank Garvin, who was going to save my brother. It seemed amazing.

We pulled up to the hospital where my brother had been born. Hank ignored my sister and me and picked up my brother and was already running through the hospital doors as Lynn and I stepped down from the truck. We hurried after Hank.

By the time we got inside, Sam lay on a gurney and was being rushed away. Hank watched. We stood beside him. He smiled at us. "He's going to be fine," he said. Lynn hugged me.

The hospital called our parents. Hank sat in the waiting room with us. Once, he looked at his watch and left the room to make a phone call. When he returned, he had a coloring book and a few broken crayons for me. I was a little old for that, but I said thank you and pretended to be absorbed in coloring. Every so often I peeked at Hank Garvin. White people were not really mean to me, but they were rarely nice, either. And here was Hank, acting like we were the most important people in the world. I decided that besides being a handsome millionaire and a karate expert, my future husband Joe-John Abondondalarama would help out people in need, just like Hank. Maybe he wouldn't even *be* a millionaire.

Even after my parents arrived, Hank still didn't leave. He waited until Sam was released. We all went up to Sam's room to get him. The doctor had said we were lucky the trap hadn't broken any bones. My father's face contorted when he saw Sam's bandaged leg. My mother kept asking the doctor what she could do, and the doctor kept saying, "It's all under control now."

We took Sam into the lobby, where my parents thanked Hank profusely. I found myself embarrassed at the smells emanating from my mother. Back in Sam's room the doctor had sniffed once at the air and looked around for the source of the smell. What the doctor smelled was my mother's pad that she hadn't had time to change. But if Hank noticed, he didn't let on. He didn't sniff the air or anything. He showed Sam a disappearing coin trick, and then he left.

Sam and Lynn rode with my father, and I rode with my mother. I knew I would be in trouble for the way the picnic had gone. I was afraid to mention our bicycles, still lying in the grass. Lynn wouldn't be in trouble because she was sick, and Sam wouldn't be in trouble because he was hurt. I waited to hear how I would be punished. Instead, my mother did not speak a word. She looked terrible. The whole car smelled from her pad, but I didn't open the window because she might be insulted.

At home later my mother gave my father and me sardines and rice. Even though Lynn was sick tonight, Sam was allowed in the bedroom. He and Lynn went to sleep. I was tired of sardines and rice and just picked at my food. My father was silent, not the normal type of quietness that I expected from him, but a dark, smoky, angry silence that I had never seen before.

"You've got a long day tomorrow," said my mother.

All my father's days were long. He worked seven days a week, every week. He hadn't taken a vacation the whole time we'd lived in Georgia. My father seemed to remember about his hard day tomorrow, and his smoky anger faded. My mother looked at me. "Clean up and get to bed. Tomorrow I want you girls to see how much money you've saved. We have to get something for that Ginger and especially that Hank Garvin."

"We hardly have any money saved."

My mother's face darkened, and my father stepped forward. "We'll get 'em something good."

"Dad?" I said. "Our bicycles are still out there. I'm sorry."

There was a long pause. I saw how exhausted my father was. "I'll go get them," he finally said.

I lay awake on my cot for a long time. I wanted to hear when my father got home. When he returned, my mother met him at the door. "They're gone," he said tiredly.

"Well, we can't afford new ones."

Their voices moved farther away. Late into

the night I could hear my parents sitting in the kitchen talking, on and on, and I knew they were talking about us kids, in the way they could talk about us endlessly and never get bored. Sometimes it seemed that one way or another, no matter what my father was saying, he was talking about us. He was talking about all the things he could do for us—and, more often, all the things he could not.

chapter 12 きらきら

LYNN DIDN'T RETURN to school in the fall. My parents told me it was her anemia, but when I looked up "anemia" in our new dictionary, this is what I found: *a condition in which the level of hemoglobin in the blood is below the normal range and there is a decrease in the production of red blood cells, often causing pallor and fatigue.* Pallor and fatigue didn't seem bad enough to make someone miss so much school.

Then Lynn was hospitalized in a nearby, bigger town for part of October. Some days, when my mother spent the day and night at the hospital, my father brought Sammy and me to the hatchery with him. A few times we slept overnight at the hatchery. There was a TV in a back room, so we watched that and read our books all day. We didn't even go to school some days. We didn't take as many baths. My parents could have arranged for us to stay at our aunt and uncle's house and go to school, but they didn't. It was as if my father didn't even want us to attend classes, because he wanted us there with him, where he knew we were safe.

The hatchery was a big, concrete, windowless building in the middle of a beautiful field. Unlike at the poultry factory, we could come and go freely at the hatchery. All we had to do was wash the bottoms of our shoes in soapy water each time we went inside. The sexers wore surgical masks so they wouldn't inhale the dusty down from the baby chicks.

I'd been excited to see all the baby chicks. The workers tolerated me and Sammy as we walked through the sexers' workroom. We got to touch the male chicks, because nobody cared about them. Each one looked different:

skinny, fat, all yellow, yellow and brown, big, small.

During the breaks we would sit outside with the sexers. Most of them smoked, and they all seemed tired all the time. Even my father seemed tired, too tired even for me and Sammy. One break we sat next to a young sexer blowing smoke rings. When he finished one cigarette, he would light another. He looked at me and Sammy.

"How'd you kids like to make yourselves helpful?"

"What do you mean?" I said.

"Billy has a guy who comes around just to get his coffee and bring him refreshments. You know who Billy is?"

"No."

"He's the best sexer in Georgia. He won the national competition in Japan before he moved to the States. He can sex twelve hundred chicks an hour with one hundred percent accuracy."

I guessed that was really good. One of the other sexers said, "Billy Morita." He shook his head admiringly.

"How many can you do an hour?"

"A thousand, ninety-eight percent accuracy."

Another sexer said, "Hey, yeah, you kids could light our cigarettes and bring us coffee."

I looked to my father to see what he thought, but he was staring into space, in another world. "Okay," I said.

So when they started working again, Sammy and I kept busy bringing them coffee, scratching their backs, lighting their cigarettes in the break room, and so on. Our father saw we were having fun. I could tell once that under his mask he was smiling. Our father was the only one who didn't ask us for anything, but we brought him things anyway. We always brought him coffee when it was the freshest and hottest, and when one of the hatchery assistants bought doughnuts, we saved our father a jelly one, because we knew that was his favorite.

There were several incubators and hatchers where the eggs stayed warm until the chicks were born. When they opened the incubators, we got to look in and see hundreds of thousands of white eggs. The warm air rushed out—the temperature had to stay at around ninety-nine degrees. On another day we got to look into the hatchers and see hundreds of thousands of yellow chicks. As soon as the chicks were born, the sexers hurried to separate the males from the females. The sexers worked for twelve hours in a row, and then they slept while a new batch of eggs warmed. They would wake up a few hours later, when the new batch was born.

The sexers got paid half a penny for each chick. Most of them had gone to school in Chicago or Japan to get this job. Chicken sexing was invented in Japan. Then a Japanese man came to Chicago and started a school to teach Japanese Americans how to sex chickens. That's where my father had learned, before he and my mother opened their store. He'd worked at a hatchery before I was born, but the work at that hatchery was seasonal, and once I was born, he needed to make more money.

The inoculators were all white women. They stuck needles full of medicine into the female chickens, so the females wouldn't get sick and die. Angel was kind of the inoculators' boss. Angel was a big burly woman with bandages around her ankles because she said standing all day hurt her legs.

The first day we visited, Sammy and I shyly watched her work. Finally, I had to ask her something.

"Does the needle hurt them?"

"Beg pardon?"

"Does it hurt the chicks when you stick the needle into them?"

"Honey, do I look like I can talk to chickens?" I didn't know how to answer that. She softened. "I don't think it hurts them unless you accidentally break their neck. That happens sometimes."

I looked into a garbage can and saw a couple of limp chicks inside. Sammy started to look inside too, but I pulled him away. I couldn't do anything about the chicks, but at least I could protect Sammy from seeing them.

I took him into the back room. Even in there, we could hear the racket from hundreds of thousands of chicks chirping. We watched

TV until my eyes hurt. Then I dressed Sammy in his soldier pajamas, and I put on my pajamas with the lace collar that my mother had made for me.

When all the sexers came in to sleep, most of them looked at Sammy and me and smiled the way Lynn smiled at us when she thought we were being delightfully immature and young. One gray-faced old sexer said to me, "Good night, Miss Lacy." He laughed as if he were quite funny. I smiled politely. The grown-ups didn't even change clothes. They just got in their sleeping bags and fell asleep. All of us slept in the same room together. Except for the gray-faced old sexer, no one even said good night to anyone else. I think they were too tired.

My father got to sleep for only four hours before it was time to go back to work. When I saw him getting ready for work, I said, "How come you have to get up now?"

"Because the chickens are ready now," he said.

I went back to sleep. It was storming outside; the hatchery manager had told the sexers that there was a tornado warning. I liked being in a warm room, any warm room, when it stormed. I wished Lynn could be with us. Maybe I would not like the storm so much if I had to lie in a hospital room, even if I was warm and my mother was with me. Just as I was drifting off I heard shouting from the main part of the hatchery. I searched the wall for the light switch but couldn't find it. I couldn't even find the crack from under the door. In a minute, though, I found the door and opened it. Outside was completely dark, but several people were shouting.

"Get a flashlight!" yelled one man.

"Why didn't the backup go on?" said another.

A flashlight came on, and I followed its light to the incubator room. The hatchery manager's face screwed up into one big scrunched-up frown. I saw my father in the dim light and walked over to him. He and the other sexers had taken down their masks. Their room was dark. My father put an arm around me.

"What happened?" I said.

"The power's out, and the backup generator's not working. If the incubators cool off for too long, they may lose part of the hatch."

"You mean the baby chicks will die?"

"Or come out deformed."

"Should I call Mr. Lyndon?" called out a man.

Everyone fell silent.

Finally, the hatchery manager said grimly, "Not yet."

"Who're we going to get to fix the generator at this hour?"

Another silence.

The hatchery manager went to a phone, and we could hear him talking softly. After awhile all he was saying was "Yes, sir," over and over. We all sat in the incubator room so our heat would keep the room warm. Before long we heard a siren in the distance. Then a sheriff entered with the man to fix the backup generator.

"Power's out all over the county," said the sheriff.

My father sent me to bed. I lay next to Sammy in the total darkness. Mr. Lyndon must have been a pretty powerful person to get a man to fix his generator *and* get a sheriff's escort in the middle of the night. That's what I was thinking about as I fell asleep.

In the morning the storm had ended. I lay in bed until Sammy woke up. That took several hours. I just lay there and thought about every single thing I could think of that had ever happened to me. It was the longest I ever stayed still in my life. I thought about the Chinese lady in Iowa who could take her teeth out, about driving to Georgia, about a boy at school who was kind of cute. I thought about Lynn being sick. For everything in my life, I would ask, *Why?* Why didn't the Chinese lady have teeth? Probably it was because she didn't brush them enough. I asked myself why we had to move to Georgia. It was because my father needed to work at this hatchery so he could support us better. Why did I kind of like that boy? Because he was kind of cute. And why was Lynnie sick? Why? There was no answer to that.

Later that day I stole a couple of male chickens and set them down in the field. "Be

free!" I said. Sammy and I walked across the
street, to a pecan grove, and picked up nuts
from the ground. Sammy had crazy bizarre
teeth like rocks, and he would crack the nut-
shells so we could eat the insides. I remembered when we first arrived in Georgia and I
saw all the mansions and all the fruit and nut
trees. I thought almost everything would
look beautiful like this pecan grove. I
thought that there would be mansions and
orchards everywhere and that nuts and fruit
would fall down and roll through the streets
whenever the wind blew the trees. I thought
that maybe at first nobody would like Lynn
but that once everybody got to know her, she
would be the most popular girl in her class
and be homecoming queen someday in high
school. And I still thought this might be pos-
sible for her.

On Halloween night my parents brought
my brother and me to visit her in the hospital.
I was dressed as a fairy godmother. I pulled
glitter off my dress and threw it over Lynnie
and said, *"Kira-kira!"* She was thin and pale,
with circles under her eyes. The glitter fell in

a sparkly rain all around her. She smiled.

My parents smiled, but weakly. They were tired. To pay Lynn's medical bills and our new mortgage, my father worked almost constantly. When he was home, all he thought about was Lynn. Our whole lives revolved around what Lynn wanted, what was good for Lynn, and what more we could do for Lynn.

Lynn came home the first week of November, on a rainy Saturday. We had decorated her room and put up a streamer that said WELCOME HOME. We'd bought the streamer at a store. It was the same color as Christmas tinsel. In the store it had seemed beautiful, but with Lynn lying in bed so pale and sick, the streamer seemed all wrong. My father took it down silently.

We quickly formed a ritual. Every night after my mother washed Lynn down, the whole family sat in our bedroom while I read to Lynn from the encyclopedia set my father had bought her for her birthday in September. It was used and it wasn't *Encyclopædia Britannica*—we couldn't afford that—but Lynn loved it anyway. As she always had been, Lynn was obsessed with the ocean, especially the ocean by California. I read anything in the encyclopedia set we could think of that concerned the ocean. She liked to know about everything, from the most peaceful tiny fish to the hungriest shark. Lynn thought it was all fascinating, and so did I. Some nights after I read, she wanted my parents to leave, and she and I talked about the houses we would live in someday by the sea. Our houses would boast huge picture windows, and palm trees would grow in our front yards. Then I would go into the living room and sleep on my cot next to the couch.

Sometimes I played hooky to be with Lynn. I wrote fake excuse letters from my mother to show the teacher, and sometimes when the teacher asked me directly what was wrong with me, I lied and said I'd had a fever the previous day. At home I read the encyclopedia to Lynn or combed her hair or painted her nails. One day she looked very sad and told me she wished she had some glittery pink polish. I didn't have any money, but I walked down to the five-and-ten store. I'd decided to steal Lynn some polish. I'd never stolen anything before, but it couldn't be hard.

When I arrived at the store, nobody was there except a lady at the front cash register. She was reading a magazine.

First I looked around the aisle where they kept bandages and antiseptic. Then I pretended to be interested in tennis shoes a couple of aisles down. Finally, I approached the nail polish. Nobody was in that aisle. This was too easy! I stuck some beautiful pink polish in my pocket and walked calmly out. I smiled as I walked through the door. It had been raining earlier, and a rainbow filled the sky. The sky was beautiful! Suddenly, I felt a hand grab my upper arm. I didn't even turn to look—I wrested my arm away and ran and ran. I kept waiting for someone to catch up with me, but no one ever did. I never looked back.

At home I painted Lynn's nails shimmery pink. She seemed so pleased, I didn't regret what I'd done. But before I got in bed later that night, I hung out the alcove window and looked up and down the street for the sheriff. The street was empty, so I slept peacefully.

The next morning before I left for school, I checked on Lynn. She was sound asleep, but her arms hung outside the blanket. Her nails looked pretty, and she was smiling slightly.

I hated to wake her up, but I had to, to give her her medicine. Eventually, when she got better, maybe some days I would let her slide and not force her to take her medicine. A part of me regretted making her miserable in this way—I think some of her pills made her feel even more awful than she already felt. Some days I think she was really miserable, because she cried a lot. In a way, I'd had to steel my heart to her crying. You need to steel yourself to a lot of things when someone in your family is really sick. I was going to give Lynn every chance to get better no matter how miserable it made her. I shook her awake.

"It's time for your pills!"

"Do I have to?"

"Yes."

She groaned softly as I propped her up. I never even asked her why she groaned, never asked her what exactly hurt when I did that. I didn't even know what made her hurt and what, if anything, made her feel good. All I knew was that my parents were at work, and it was my job to give her some pills.

I waited until she swallowed her water. Then I gently laid her back down. I got Sammy ready for school and called Mrs. Kanagawa, who sat with Lynnie during the days. As I was leaving she'd turned her head a bit and was admiring her pretty nails. I was in a good mood all day and was even able to answer a question during history.

When I got home, my mother was already there for some reason. She was talking to a white woman I had never seen. As soon as I walked through the doorway, the woman said, "That's her."

My mother bowed a slight bow to the woman and said, "I'm very sorry." She reached into her wallet. "Let me pay for it."

The woman took a dollar from her. "Will she be punished?"

"Yes, she certainly will."

The woman nodded. She walked out, glaring at me along the way. Right before she walked out, she said, "Shame on you!"

As soon as the woman left, my mother burst into tears. "My family is falling apart," she cried out. She ran out of the room.

I felt guilty then. I immediately went to my work area in the alcove and started to do my homework. When Silly's mother or uncle could drive her, she would come over for a couple of hours in the afternoons and help me with my homework. Like my sister, Silly was a straight-A student. I was doing even worse than usual at school that semester, and they were already talking about holding me back if I didn't improve.

Tonight I was supposed to write a book report on *The Call of the Wild*. It was my most favorite book I ever read, so I thought the report would be easy. The question we were supposed to answer in our report was: What is the theme of *The Call of the Wild*? What *was* the theme? I could never figure out exactly what "theme" meant. I wrote down that the theme was that dogs were loyal to good people. *Furthermore*, I wrote, *dogs are good pets to own because of their loyalty. Loyalty is the theme. That is a fine theme.* What else? *In Alaska you need a dog to pull your sled. This proves that dogs and man were meant to be friends. This is another theme of* The Call of the Wild.

Then I walked with Sam over to our former apartment to watch TV with Mrs. Muramoto. We watched until bedtime and returned home. When we came through the door, my mother was waiting. "Your father is in the kitchen. He wants to talk to you."

This was a very bad sign. He had never given me a talk. Lynn, of course, used to give me big talks. And my mother had given me a talk earlier that year, about what would happen when I started menstruating. And the vice principal had recently given me a talk about how if you got on the wrong track in grade school, you might never get off and you would end up either in a terrible job or else married to someone with a terrible job.

I sat down at our table in the kitchen. My father, reading the newspaper, ignored me at first. I examined a chip on our yellow Formica table. Our chairs were green. A neighbor had given us the table, and our uncle had given us the chairs. Nothing in our house matched.

My father set his paper down and looked at me. "Lynn does have anemia," he said. "But she also has lymphoma, and it's very serious." He seemed to be thinking hard. "Tomorrow I want you to go to the store and apologize for stealing that nail polish."

"Okay."

"I know you're a good girl," he said. "I've always known that. But sometimes I like to see it, just to remind me. You think you could remind me of that a little more often?"

"Yes. What's lymphoma?"

"It's a very bad disease. But your sister's going to get better. Now that we have the house, she's happier."

I went to the bedroom. Lynn was sleeping, as usual. I looked up "lymphoma" in the dictionary. It took me fifteen minutes just to figure out how to spell it. The dictionary said: *Any of the various malignant tumors that arise in the lymph nodes or in other lymphoid tissue.* Then I looked up "malignant" in the dictionary. It said: *Threatening to life; virulent: a malignant disease. Tending to metastasize; cancerous. Used of a tumor.*

And that was how I found out Lynn might die.

I turned to her and stared. As she slept she looked a lot like she'd looked when she was well. I still thought she was beautiful, and so was her hair. But I couldn't help noticing that her hair and skin were not as beautiful as they once had been, and she seemed thin.

The manager of the dime store was a small, balding man who gestured a lot with his hands. After I apologized to him, he lectured me about the black sheep of his family. I think I was just about the most lectured-to girl in Georgia at that point.

The black sheep in the manager's family was named Oscar, and he had been in and out of reform school as a teenager and in and out of jail as a grown-up. The manager showed me a mug shot of Oscar. He said that Oscar had started out on his life of crime by going on a shoplifting spree when he was my age. This talk was kind of a surprise to me. I doubted I would ever go to jail, so that part of the lecture didn't scare me. But I wondered whether I could end up the black sheep of my family. We didn't really have a black sheep. In other words, the job was open.

Of course, I didn't tell Lynn about stealing the nail polish. That night I got up in the middle of the night and took my blanket into the bedroom so that I could sleep on the floor next to Lynn's bed. My mother still wanted Sammy and me to stay in the living room so that we wouldn't bother Lynn. I didn't think we were bothering her, but when my mother stepped on me in the middle of the night while checking on Lynn, she sent me back to my cot. I watched the dim motel light flashing on the living-room wall. When my mother went back to sleep, I returned to the floor next to Lynn's bed. I decided I would sleep like that every night until . . . well, every night until she got better.

In fact, some days she was better. That is, she wasn't well, but some days she got up and ate dinner with us. On those days we competed with one another to take care of her. If we even suspected she might want more water or milk or green beans or anything at all, we would run to the kitchen to get what she wanted.

When she wasn't so well, my mother and I put her on a sheet. We would each take an end of the sheet and carry her outside, where she liked to lie on her very own grass on her very own yard and stare at the sky, day or night, it didn't matter. She belonged to the sky, and the sky belonged to her. Then one day when we brought her out, I saw that her eyes were glazed as she stared at the bright blueness of the sky. On that day the sky seemed to mean nothing to her. The next day was the same.

chapter 13 きらきら

BECAUSE OF LYNN'S medical bills, soon my parents were getting behind on the mortgage. All they did was work. My mother came home only to sleep, and my father did not come home at all. Auntie or Mrs. Kanagawa stayed with Lynn and Sammy during the day when I was at school. My parents were so exhausted, I wasn't sure they even realized what arrangements we were making each day. Some days *nobody* stayed with us.

Most of the time Lynn slept, but anytime she was awake, she wanted attention. She wanted a bedpan, or food, or water, or some-times just a little company. But sometimes she didn't know what she wanted. In fact, it seemed that at least once a day she didn't know what she wanted. That was the most exhaust-ing thing. She would want me to read to her, and then she wouldn't like the book and would want me to read something else. And then she still wouldn't like the book and would want me to sing for her. But she wouldn't like that, either. My teacher had commented on the black circles under my eyes. A couple of morn-ings I even made myself coffee.

Sammy and I slept in the room with her now, because somebody needed to be with her all the time. Once, Lynn woke up in the middle of the night, the way she often did.

"Katie?" she said.

I almost never slept deeply anymore—as soon as she said my name, I always sat up immediately, no matter how tired I was. But that night I was completely exhausted. I could barely pull myself up.

"Katie?" she said, more impatiently.

"Uh-huh." I sat up. "Yeah, okay."

"I want some milk."

"Now? Are you sure?"

"What do you mean, am I sure? I want some milk."

I got up and went to the kitchen and brought back a glass of milk. I pulled her up and picked up the bolster from the floor and used it to support her back. She took one sip of milk and made a face. "Can I have water instead?"

"I thought you said you were sure!"

She looked as if she might cry. "I said I'm thirsty!" She dropped the cup to the floor. I just stood there a moment, watching her small rug soak up the milk.

I suddenly felt angry at her. "Dad had to buy you that rug, you know."

"I want water!"

I went to the kitchen and came back with water, a soapy dishrag, and a towel. I handed her the water without comment. Sammy's eyes were open wide, watching me. I cleaned up the rug.

Lynn cried out, "There's soap on this water glass!" She flung it to the floor.

I stared at the cup for a moment. Then I

whipped around. "You're ruining everything!" I said. "We got a new house, and you're ruining everything! Mom and Dad worked so hard to get this house. *You're* ruining it!"

She looked really hurt for a moment, but then she got angry. She said, *"I want milk."*

I said, "No."

"I *hate* you."

"I hate *you!*"

Sammy said, "Katie?"

"Shut up!" I snapped at him, and he was still.

I finished cleaning up and got in bed. Sammy was still awake, staring at me. I told him to go to sleep. Lynn started to cry, but only for about fifteen minutes.

Then she started to make a soft, mournful, squeaky noise, kind of like "heeah . . . heeah . . . heeah," every time she exhaled. She didn't sound like Lynn, she sounded like an animal. Since she never seemed to inhale deeply anymore, her breathing was quick and shallow. She made the noise on and on, weakly. She didn't cry again, she just kept making the noise. It sounded really sad.

Sammy's face looked scared in the glow from the Rabbit on the Moon night-light Auntie Fumi had given Lynn.

I ignored my sister and brother, just lay there and listened to Lynnie in the dim light. Usually while I lay in bed, I liked to think of new things I could do for Lynnie. Maybe I could let her try my pillow to see if she liked it better. Or I could bring her a new cracker she'd never tried. Or maybe I could even find a new book that she'd never heard of and read it to her, even though she had heard of every book in the world. That night I knew that nothing I could do would make her feel better. So I lay in bed and listened to her mournful noise and didn't feel love or hate or anger or anything at all except despair.

For Thanksgiving weekend my parents needed a break from me and Sammy, and we needed a break from them. No one felt like eating turkey. My parents arranged for Uncle to take us on a camping trip. He took his kids camping almost every weekend, even when it rained. He called every Friday night and asked whether we wanted to come. We always said no. I wanted to stay with Lynn. But this time my parents made me go.

We left early on a Saturday morning. My parents seemed relieved to see us go. It made me surprised and guilty to find how glad I felt to get out of the house where everything reminded me of my sister. I felt guilty whenever I left my sister's side, but at the same time I could not be with her every moment. If I had been, I would have lost my mind. Maybe I *was* losing my mind. Sometimes, even just for three minutes, even when it was my turn to be with Lynnie, I had to step outside. I had to look at the sky. I had to be anywhere else but in that sad room with her.

In addition to Sammy and me, Uncle was bringing his family, my friend Silly, and his friend Jedda-Boy, a local land surveyor. Silly and I rode in the truck with Uncle. Amazingly, it was the same truck he had driven us to Georgia in years earlier. It didn't go more than twenty-five miles an hour, so Jedda-Boy's truck lost us in the first ten minutes. Unfortunately, Uncle had never been to our destination before. We were going to one of Jedda-Boy's favorite campsites. Uncle got lost and refused to stop for directions because, he kept saying, he knew the way, which he obviously didn't.

At one point we went down a small road that ended at a cliff. The truck got stuck and wouldn't back up. I could literally see down into a canyon before us. If we went forward, we would fall to our deaths. Then Lynn would miss me and might get sicker. Uncle wanted Silly and me to sit in the truck bed to get better traction. So she and I got in back and prayed that my uncle wouldn't go forward by accident.

The truck revved and revved and shook and shook, but it was still stuck. Then Uncle tried to explain to me how to use a clutch, so that I could back up the truck while he and Silly sat in the bed, since he was heavier than I was and would give us better traction. I couldn't figure out the clutch. In fact, at one point while I was learning, the truck jolted forward several inches. Uncle screamed a scream as high-pitched as a girl's and rammed his foot on top of mine on the brake. He taught Silly instead.

She was like Lynn in that she could do anything, including crazy stuff like learning how to use a clutch.

Uncle and I climbed in back. Silly turned once to look at us. She crossed her fingers and then turned forward. The truck shook and rattled, and then we backed up.

Uncle was sweating. He seemed to think we would all be dead if he hadn't slammed his foot on mine. My toes still hurt. He looked at me with new respect, I guess over just how much trouble I was capable of causing. He got in and started driving again. We pulled around a corner, and I felt myself totter uncertainly and then lean into the door. He'd told me the door came loose sometimes. I tried to stop myself, but the door fell open. The next thing I knew, my back was scraping along rocks on the roadside.

Unbelievably, no one noticed, not even Silly. They rolled merrily along while I lay on the road and watched the truck recede. I screamed, "Wait for me!" In a moment the truck came slowly down the road from the opposite direction. I saw Silly point at me excitedly, and the truck pulled over. I got in the truck and refused to talk to Uncle Katsuhisa. My shirt was torn in back. Basically, there were already about a thousand things I could snitch on Uncle for if I wanted.

He seemed to realize that, because he handed me a piece of rice candy and said, "I'd like to give you this." I continued to shun him. "All right, then, here," he said. He handed me the whole pack of rice candy plus a Hershey's bar. I took the rice candy, handing the Hershey's bar to Silly.

"Now, don't you tell your parents you fell out of the truck."

"I won't."

He shook his head. "I still remember when I could bribe you for half a stick of gum."

At the campgrounds Jedda-Boy had already set up camp. When I started to tell the story of the cliff, Uncle frowned at me, so I didn't say anything. He smiled innocently at Auntie Fumi.

David, Daniel, Silly, and I ran off to play a game we called Hunter and Hunted with water guns. At first I hadn't felt like playing, but they begged me. Silly and I chose to be the deer first; David and Daniel would hunt us with their water guns. I found I loved pretending to be a deer, loping through the forest as the boys counted to one hundred. Silly and I moved as quickly and quietly as we could. We had to balance our movements between speed and noise. Silly was like an animal, with perfect animal instincts about where to go and how to move gracefully. We heard David and Daniel call out, "Here we come, deer!"

I thought I could feel the blood rushing through my body. For a moment I forgot I was human. We moved very quietly. Then we stopped moving and just listened. We couldn't hear a thing. Suddenly, there was a huge crashing nearby, and we crashed away in the opposite direction. I found myself laughing crazily as I ran. I felt so free!

Silly and I split up in different directions. I heard Daniel yelling, "I'll get Silly!" I ran desperately through the woods. There was a sudden open area, and I ran and ran across. I felt like a real deer, graceful and fast. I saw an arc of water by my side. It missed me! Then water splattered on my head. I collapsed to the ground and groaned the way I thought an animal might. David ran up and put his foot on my stomach and pounded his chest and said, "For I am the greatest hunter *alive*!"

We turned to watch Silly running into the woods chased by Daniel. In a minute he came out of the woods looking confused. He stood still to listen. David and I helped him look for Silly. About ten minutes later we still hadn't found her. Daniel yelled, "Ollie, Ollie, ocean free!" Silly appeared right where we'd just come from. I was so proud of her.

Then it was the boys' turn to be the deer. They went to hide. We didn't chase them. Instead, we returned to camp to play cards in our tent. We were so funny! When the boys finally figured out where we were, they refused to speak to us. So we refused to speak to them.

David said, "How can you not speak to us when you're the ones who played the trick?" But we didn't answer because we weren't speaking to them!

When night approached, Uncle made us a fire, and I lay near it and felt the heat on my body. I stared at the sky, as I had done so many times with my sister. I was surprised to realize that I hadn't thought of my sister for nearly an hour—the whole time we were playing and about half an hour after. That was the longest I hadn't thought about her for a while. I felt refreshed, as if I could now sit with her for ten years straight if necessary to help her get well.

Auntie and Sam sat next to me. David, Daniel, and Silly were playing some game. Uncle and Jedda-Boy took a couple of surveying instruments and discussed mud and sand and other important surveying matters. Jedda-Boy was talking about how once when he lived in Nevada, he got helicoptered to a secret location to measure some land. The land was in the desert near where nuclear bomb tests had been held. He finished the job even though the area was probably radioactive, because a self-respecting surveyor always finishes a job no matter what it involves, including, he said, wild dogs, gunshots from angry neighbors mixed up in a property dispute, snakes and alligators, and radioactivity.

I said quietly, "Auntie, when is Uncle Katsuhisa going to quit his job at the hatchery and become a land surveyor?"

She pushed back my hair and said sadly, "Sweetheart, nobody in Georgia is going to hire a Japanese man to be a land surveyor."

"How do you know?"

"He's been turned down for five jobs."

"But he can be whatever he wants. Lynn is going to be either a rocket scientist or a famous writer."

"It's different for you children. You're younger, the world is changing."

Jedda-Boy was talking loudly. "The first time I got chased by an alligator, I was scared, I admit that. But I finished the job later."

Sammy smiled serenely and looked at the beautiful sky. Lynn liked to say the stars were the ultimate thing you could describe as *kira-kira*. The second most ultimate thing was the way the sun glittered off the ocean. Of course, she had never seen this, but she could imagine exactly how it would look.

Uncle came and sat down with us. I said, "Uncle, can't you become a land surveyor?"

He drank from his canteen and wiped his mouth. He didn't answer for a long time. Everyone was quiet. After a time he said, "I remember that when I was a boy, I thought I was going to grow up and map the world."

Auntie stroked his face.

Uncle saw Sammy gazing at the sky, and he looked at the sky too. "Would you look at those stars! I can really see how the ancient Egyptians or whoever the hell it was said, 'Goddamnit, let's name those goddamn stars and go down in history!'"

I didn't know what the ancient Egyptians had said, but I doubted they had said exactly that.

Uncle's face got wistful as he stared into the sky. Auntie kissed his face. He put his arm around her, and they leaned against each other. I saw in their faces how happy they were, and sad, too, because Uncle Katsuhisa would never be a land surveyor.

New Year's is the biggest holiday of the year for the Japanese. Every year since we'd lived in Georgia, Mrs. Muramoto held a big party. She served *sake* and *mochi* and a couple dozen different snacks. We would usually stay until about ten and then go home. Just before dawn I would get up and write down my *hatsu-yume*, first dream of the new year. Then we would meet the other families and go to the empty lot nearby with our lawn chairs to watch the sunrise. Watching the first sunrise is the traditional way to celebrate New Year's in Japan. The last few years, though, nobody had bothered getting up for the sunrise. The fathers were all too tired for such a celebration.

Mrs. Kanagawa stayed with Lynn and Sammy while I went to Mrs. Muramoto's for just half an hour before returning to sit with Lynn. Mrs. Kanagawa told me Lynn had been very peaceful. We made quiet small talk about the party, and then Mrs. Kanagawa left. Lynn continued to sleep, her breath catching heart-breakingly, as if breathing had become a hard-ship for her body. Her hair had grown stringy. I moved a strand of hair from her forehead, then pulled a chair to the window and spied on Mr. and Mrs. Miller's party next door. It was quite a bit noisier than the party at Mrs.

Muramoto's. Everybody seemed drunk. All at once the men started to put bows on their foreheads and run out the front door. I had no idea what they were doing. I hurried into the alcove and peeked out our front window. The men ran down the street shouting "Happy New Year!" with the bows on their foreheads. Even though I was in a sad mood, I couldn't help smiling at these crazy white people.

I went into the kitchen and called my parents at the party and told them Lynn was sleeping peacefully. Someday when Lynn got better, we were going to get her a phone for the bedroom. Gregg and Amber both used to call all the time, so when she got better and made more friends, she would need a phone.

I put on my pajamas around 11:30 and lay on the floor next to Lynn's bed. The Rabbit on the Moon looked so pretty shining in the outlet.

"Katie?" Lynn said softly. She hadn't talked all day.

I sat up. "Yes?"

"You have to try to get better grades. Promise?"

"Okay."

"You should go to college. Promise?"

"I'll think about it."

"Promise?"

"Yes."

"Take care of Mom and Dad and Sammy."

"Okay, I promise." I hesitated. "When you get better, you can help me take care of them."

"Okay, I promise." She laughed very softly, almost soundlessly.

The phone rang, and she seemed to perk up a bit. But it stopped after just one ring, and she seemed to deflate. It was amazing that as sick as she was, she could still be interested in something as small as the ring of a phone.

She groaned suddenly. "Can we open the window?"

I jumped up to open the window. She closed her eyes, and I sat next to the bed and stared at her. Her skin looked almost purely white, like the white of the ghost of Brenda I'd seen at the swamp. She opened her eyes again.

"It's too dark in here," she said.

I turned on the light. A little brown moth flitted in. It wasn't big, not even an inch long.

It landed on the ceiling. Lynn stared at it. Then it flitted toward the lamp and away again. Lynn kept watching. For a moment the party next door quieted down. Our room was so quiet, I could just make out the sound of the moth's wings. Lynn didn't move, except for her eyes. Her eyes moved this way and that as she watched the moth. It was strange because although her eyes showed no emotion or interest, she must have been interested in order to be watching the moth so closely. She couldn't take her eyes off that little bug as it sailed across the room and back again, across and back. And then I thought I saw something in her eyes, some emotion or interest, but I wasn't sure what it was.

The moth settled down, and she went to sleep. I closed my eyes and tried to sleep on the floor with the lights on. I didn't like to sleep in my bed because it was too far from Lynnie, several feet away.

For some reason my mother didn't make me go back to my cot that night. I couldn't sleep deeply, so I didn't have a *hatsu-yume*. When it was almost sunrise, I sat up and watched Lynn sleep for a few minutes. Then I took a lawn chair and a blanket down to the empty lot on the corner. I was alone. I thought about getting dressed, but I wasn't expecting to see anybody. I stared east, at the giant tire over the tire store across from the lot. The giant tire looked just like the giant doughnut over the doughnut store on Main Street, except that the tire was black and the dough-nut was brown.

It was cold out. Here are the sounds I heard:

1. An old piece of newspaper flutter-ing in the breeze.
2. A mechanical whirring—I didn't know what was making that sound.
3. A bird chirping.
4. A quick *click-clicking* from a bug light at the tire store.

We lived below what Georgians called the gnat line, meaning all the gnats in the world lived in town with us. My uncle claimed that more bugs lived per square mile in southern

Georgia than anywhere in the state. Even in winter, there were bugs.

Those were the only noises.

Here are the things I saw:

1. The tire store—through a window, I saw tires piled inside.
2. A lonely tree outside the store.
3. The gray sky.
4. A crow sitting on the giant tire.

I cried and cried. For a while as I cried I hated my parents, as if it were their fault that Lynn was sick. Then I cried because I loved my parents so much.

Then I didn't feel like crying anymore. I just felt barren, my eyes felt dry. The sky was still gray. Everything was gray, the sky and the store and even my hand when I held it out in front of myself. I wondered if anyone else in history had ever been as sad as I was at that moment. As soon as I wondered that, I knew the answer was yes. The answer was that millions of people had been that sad. For instance, what about the people of the great Incan city of Cuzco, which was ransacked by foreigners in the sixteenth century? I wrote a paper about that for school. And then there were all the millions of people in all the many wars throughout history and throughout the world, and all the millions of people with loved ones killed by millions of other people.

A lot of people had been as sad as I was. Maybe a billion of them had been this sad. As soon as I realized this, I felt like I was no longer a little girl but had become a big girl. What being a big girl meant exactly, I wasn't sure.

I watched a swatch of the sky turn red. The red spread like blood in the sea: red, red, red, and then less and less red, until there was only blue left. I squinted as the sun rose. I must have fallen asleep, because when I woke up, my father was carrying me into the house. Sam walked beside us carrying the lawn chair, which seemed almost as big as he was.

Inside the living room my father laid me on my cot. "She's gone," he said.

chapter 14 きらきら

I WATCHED MY father walk away. I got up and ran behind him to the doorway of the bedroom, then hesitated. My mother was weeping as she knelt by the side of the bed and leaned over my sister. My father knelt in front of the bed and enveloped Lynn's head with his arms. It was light outside now, but nobody had bothered to turn off the lamp. I stared at the lamp. The lamp was on because Lynn had asked that I turn it on, but now she herself was gone. I couldn't comprehend it. I walked in slowly. My parents scarcely noticed me. My father moved to my mother and put his arms around her.

Lynn looked peaceful, even beautiful, but slightly off. Her eyes were not quite closed all the way, and her mouth hung open a bit. My mother suddenly got up and held a mirror to Lynn's nose, apparently hoping to see a fog of breath on the mirror. But the mirror stayed clear.

"Who was with her?" I said.

My father's voice broke as he said, "Nobody."

That cut hard into me. I wished so badly that I had not gone out. I should have known better. I should have! I could not imagine what dying must have felt like for her. I had no idea whether it mattered or not to her that she had been alone at the exact moment she died. But I thought maybe it did matter.

Then there was a frenzy of activity as my parents got ready for the funeral. Though I had hardly slept, I couldn't sleep any more that day. The lack of sleep coupled with Lynnie's death made the world surreal. All day people came and went, and I kept hearing some of them call Lynn "the body." Finally, I shouted at one of them, "Stop calling her that!" After that everyone only whispered around me, but I couldn't hear what they were saying.

My mother didn't want to throw away anything that had existed while Lynn was still alive. Before Lynn's body was taken away, my mother had me cut my sister's fingernails and even her toenails and place them in an envelope. She asked me to gather Lynn's things that lay around the house. And she wanted me to make a pile of any newspapers I could find from before Lynn died, so she could always remember what was going on in the world when Lynn passed. In the afternoon I walked in the bathroom and found my mother examining hairs she found on the floor, so that she could save those hairs she determined to belong to Lynn. Finally, my mother had me go outside and search through our garbage. She wanted to make sure there was nothing regarding Lynn that she should save.

I went outside and took a bag out of our can. I poured the contents onto the driveway. I saw a neighbor watching, but I didn't care.

The sun was warm on my back. But instead of feeling like complaining, I felt my mother's fervor. I felt it was very important to find Lynnie items. There were maggots in the bag. They didn't bother me, because I had a mission. The first bag was full of treasures: a paper with a scribble I recognized as Lynn's; a newspaper from a week ago; and a pencil Lynn had chewed. I searched through three bags, full of such precious items.

Before they came for Lynn, I cut off a lock of my hair and placed it in the pocket of her pajamas. But I remembered she would wear something different than her pajamas for the cremation. So I tied the lock of my hair around her neck. Then when Lynn was gone, I lay on her bed and cried. After I cried awhile, I started to feel angry. I didn't understand why the doctor who came to make sure Lynn was dead was one of the same doctors who had been taking care of her. If he was such a good doctor, then why did she die? And I thought maybe the doctor was mistaken, my parents were mistaken, and now they had taken Lynn away when she still possessed a small spark of life in her. Miracles happen: Maybe she would open her eyes later! What if my mother had held the mirror wrong and had missed Lynn's feeble breath?

And yet I knew Lynn was dead. I could feel the place inside of me where she had resided. This place was empty.

It was hard to stay angry when I felt so sad. I would rather have felt angry, but instead, all I could do was sob. Even though people had been coming over all day, the house seemed so lonely that I couldn't stand it.

The room grew somewhat dimmer. I didn't move as it grew dimmer still. Then, with a start, I hurried outside and ran to the alley in back of our house. Through a break between the buildings, I saw that the sun hung low over the horizon. I watched it until it started to hide between two trees in the distance. Then I climbed on a car and watched until only half of the sun was visible, and then a quarter, and then I felt a huge sickening panic inside of me and ran as hard as I could to a ladder I saw down the alley. I rushed up the ladder and climbed on the roof of somebody's garage. I saw the sun again, a quarter of it, and then a slice, and then it disappeared, the last time ever that the sun would set on a day my sister had lived.

I stood on the roof and watched the darkening sky. I heard my father calling out, "Katie! Katie!" I didn't answer; I didn't want to talk to anyone. His voice grew closer and then farther away. For some reason I felt panicked again and screamed, "Dad! Daddy!" His voice grew closer: "Katie! Katie!" He sounded panicked too. I hurried down the ladder and fell into his arms. I cried and cried, and he did not cry at all.

We walked quietly inside for another meal of sardines and rice.

Sammy ate calmly. My mother ate doggedly. My father ate politely. I didn't eat at all.

"Can I fill my water glass?" said Sammy.

"Yes," said my mother.

He got up, pulled his chair over to the sink, and filled his glass. He limped a little as he walked to the sink. Usually his ankle was fine, but every so often since his accident his ankle hurt. That smoky anger I had seen once before filled my father's face. He turned to me. I thought he was mad at me for some reason. Suddenly, he stood up. "That's enough, Katie," he said.

I wasn't sure what he meant, but I jumped to my feet.

"You're going to show me where you found the trap that hurt Sammy," he said.

"Okay. Why?"

"Because if it's still there, I want to throw it away."

My mother stood up. "You want to what?"

"You heard me."

"You are taking that girl out over my dead body."

He seemed to consider this. Finally, he said, "No."

So once again I sat in a passenger seat and bumped across the fields toward where we'd held our picnic months earlier. The last time I'd been here, Lynn and I had eaten rice balls together.

An animal, maybe a coyote, scrambled across the field as we drove. I directed my father to where I thought we'd held our picnic. My father told me to wait in the car.

"Be careful, Dad," I said.

"I know," he said.

I sat there as the sky turned black and the air grew brisk. I closed the windows and leaned against the glass, watching my dad, with a flashlight on now, searching through the trees and field, his face in the flashlight's glow grim and determined and, maybe, a little crazy about this thing that had hurt his son, this thing owned by a mean rich man who owned his dream house. He left my sight for a long time, and I got nervous and even started to feel sick to my stomach, but then his light flashed somewhere different from where I'd thought he was. I didn't know what good it would do if he did find the trap, but I felt glad anyway that he was looking. I liked being out here better than being at home. I felt scared to return to that house where Lynn no longer lived. I thought I would be so sad, I would die.

When he finally returned, he threw some things into the trunk and got in. If anything, he seemed angrier than before.

"What kind of man puts traps like that in a field? What is he trying to catch?"

"Squirrels?"

He looked at me. "Squirrels?!"

He started the car suddenly, and we lurched across the field toward Mr. Lyndon's house. My heart pounded as we bumped across the grass. I thought maybe my father wanted to yell at Mr. Lyndon. This terrified me. First of all, it was as if my father had turned into a different person. Where was my real father, who always looked before he leapt? Second of all, Mr. Lyndon was, well, he was Mr. Lyndon. You couldn't just go to his house to yell at him. And shouldn't we go home to take care of my mother and Sammy?

We reached the private road in front of the mansion, and my father kept driving. He stopped not far from the house and opened up our trunk and pulled out a two-by-four. He walked up the driveway to a red Cadillac and crashed the wood into the front windshield.

Glass exploded outward and sprinkled to the ground. I thought I saw someone peek out the windows at this madman who was my father. My father got in and we roared away.

I looked at him, but his face held no

expression. Lynn once said our father was the most determined man in the world. I remembered once how she and I had seen someone act rude to our father. Later I asked her why our father didn't hit the rude man. Lynn said that he accepted rudeness and unfairness to himself, just as he accepted hard work. If he could have, he would have worked all the time and never slept. My father was the most generous man in the world. I knew that without Lynn telling me so. If Mr. Lyndon or any other man had come to our house feeling hungry, my father would have welcomed him and given him the best food in our kitchen— the freshest fish, the hottest rice, the sweetest pastries. He would have made us be polite. He would accept anything and anyone, so long as he could earn a living to help his family. But I saw that on this one day, for the first time since I'd known him, he could not accept the way his life was turning out.

I watched our small town pass by. We drove right past where we should have turned to go home. We didn't stop until we were in the next town. Then my father pulled over and lay back against his car seat. I didn't move. He was my father, but I was not sure whether he was sane. Since Lynn had been sick, he'd been grumpier, but I'd never seen anything like tonight.

He studied me.

"Hungry?" he said.

"Uh-huh."

"Yeah, I know you are."

Our car suddenly filled with light, and then a sheriff's car pulled in front of us. The sheriff got out and slowly walked over. He shone a flashlight at us. My father rolled down the window.

"Going for a ride?" said the sheriff.

My father hesitated. I saw that he suddenly couldn't think. I felt a protective surge. I'd never felt before that I had to protect my father. But now I needed to protect him against this man. The only thing I could think to say was, "We're on our way to eat tacos!"

"Tacos?" said the sheriff. He looked confused. "You mean at Pepe's?"

"Yes, sir," I said, though I had never heard of Pepe's. As a matter of fact, I'd eaten tacos only once, years earlier in a restaurant in Illinois. I have no idea why I came up with tacos.

The sheriff studied my father. "We just had an incident at Mr. Lyndon's house."

"Oh?" said my father.

"Someone busted up his Caddy."

"Oh."

The sheriff shone the light on me. "They think the perpetrator drove a light blue Ford." Our Oldsmobile was gray, light gray. The sheriff moved his light over the outside of our gray car. My father leaned out and said, "I've always been an Oldsmobile man."

The sheriff leaned in with his light shining on me. I smiled, but he could tell I'd been crying. "Something the matter?" he said.

"My sister died," I said. I let out a sob.

He turned off the light. He seemed to think. The night had grown cool, and when he breathed through his mouth, mist filled the air in front of his face. He switched on the flashlight again and pointed it at my father. He turned it off again. He straightened up and nodded at my father. "Better get her some tacos."

We drove off in a new direction and stopped at a small Mexican restaurant called Pepe's. I didn't say anything, but I felt pretty surprised at this new turn of events. I had loved tacos the one time I ate them. But it was weird to eat them now, in my saddest moment.

The floor of the restaurant was made of brick-colored tiles, and all the tables were covered with pretty blue-and-white tile. Ponchos and sombreros hung on the walls. A singer crooned in Spanish from the record player. The atmosphere was festive. A waiter approached us and said, "Dinner for two, amigo?"

The night didn't seem real. My sister was dead, and I was about to eat tacos. I ordered five of them. In Illinois, I had eaten one. Now I ate all five of my tacos while my father watched, impressed and then maybe a little worried. "You don't want to get indigestion," he said.

When we got home, my mother was sewing a hem in the kitchen. She was fixing my black dress that I knew I would be wearing to the funeral.

"I was worried," she said.

"Katie ate five tacos," said my dad. "That takes time."

He and my mother both looked at my stomach as if expecting to see it explode. When it didn't explode, my mother raised her eyes to my father. She said the thing she liked to say when she wanted to remind him that he could not afford any sort of unusual behavior. "You've got a long day tomorrow."

He and my mother left the kitchen. She didn't ask me to wash the dishes. And she didn't do them herself. I had never known my mother to go to sleep with a sink full of dirty dishes. And I never washed them myself unless I'd been nagged. But that night I thought I should. I cleaned the counters and even took a mop to the floor. I wasn't sure what sponge to use for the counters. It seemed to me that my mother used a different sponge depending on what she was doing. But there was only one sponge at the sink. An array of bottles and jars of cleaning fluids sat under the sink. But there were no more sponges. I could imagine my mother getting annoyed if I used the wrong sponge. If Lynn were here, she would have been able to tell me what sponge I should have used, she would have been able to tell me what I should do next. I did not know what to do without her to tell me. I lowered my head to the kitchen table and cried. Finally I wet a dishtowel and used that to clean the counters, the table, and even the chair seats. It was late when I finished. I sat at our table and did not know what to do next.

Later on I lay in bed and saw the happy little moth, still alive, flitting from the night-light up the wall and back to the night-light. And it occurred to me what I had seen in Lynn's eyes the night before: She was wishing she were that moth. Maybe that was the last thing she ever wished.

chapter 15 きらきら

WE WERE HOLDING the services at the funeral home. I was supposed to give one of the eulogies because everybody said Lynn loved me more than anything in the world. I thought every spare moment about my speech. I also needed to write an essay for school about a family subject or theme, so I decided to make my speech the same as my essay. But I couldn't even think of the first sentence. I looked up "theme" in Lynn's dictionary. It said: *an implied idea in a work of art.* I thought about that for a while, and then I gave up.

My parents were busy, and Sam was sleeping. When she was a girl, my mother had dreamed of owning a flower shop, so she drew dozens of diagrams of how she might organize and display the flowers for the funeral. My father took care of all the arrangements that required dealing with the outer world, all the arrangements with the funeral home, and so on.

It made me sad that the girls from Lynn's class didn't show up for the funeral. All thirty-two Japanese in town showed up, including a new baby. In addition, Lynn's teacher from school attended. Silly, her mother, her uncle, and her brother also attended. So did Hank Garvin and his wife and kids. His wife wore a button on her lapel that said UNION, and I noticed Hank Garvin wore the inexpensive watch that was the best we could afford to give him for a thank-you. A couple of my mother's co-workers also showed up. One of them had a black eye. I'd heard that there had been union trouble at the factory, but I didn't know the details.

I couldn't pay much attention to what was

going on because I was so nervous about my speech. I was supposed to go up after Lynn's teacher. I don't even remember what she said. When it was my turn, I noticed that my shoes squeaked as I walked up the aisle. The pulpit seemed to be about a thousand miles away. *Squeak. Squeak. Squeak.* I wished the organ player would play music so nobody could hear my shoes.

Here is the speech I gave:

"My sister was my best friend. She was a genius. She helped me with my homework whenever I wanted. She was going to college and planned to live on the highest floor of a tall building, probably in Chicago. She was going to live in a house in California by the sea because she loved the sea, even though she never saw it. She was going to buy seven houses for my parents, if they wanted. She was going to be either a rocket scientist or a famous writer.

"She was going to be the best in the world and live at the top of everything, and she was going to bring her family with her. This was one of the themes of my sister's life."

My mother had told me to end with a special memory I had of my sister. But when I checked my index cards, I saw that I hadn't brought the cards on which I'd written my memory. Where had I left those cards? At home? In the car? I couldn't even recall what memory I'd planned to tell. I looked at everyone. Everyone looked at me. I cried out, "Thank you," and ran to my seat. As soon as I sat down, every single person turned to look at me. Then every single person except Silly turned forward as someone else went up to speak. Silly leaned toward me and smiled and whispered, "You were *great.*"

Later, before they buried the urn, we were each supposed to throw a flower into the hole. Almost everybody chose red roses. Uncle chose a bright yellow daisy. I chose a cosmos because my uncle told me that a cosmos stands for "heart of a girl." My father's white rose missed the hole when he threw it. He'd chosen a rose because he thought that was the most royal flower and Lynn was his little empress, and he'd chosen white because it was angelic. The white rose had landed on a mound of dirt. For a moment nobody moved. My father seemed paralyzed. Then Uncle Katsuhisa stepped forward and gently picked up the rose and threw it into the right place. He laid a hand on my father's shoulder. My father began to cry. I'd never seen my father cry before. I hadn't seen him cry the entire time since Lynn had died. Crying made his whole body shake wildly, as if he were possessed. The shaking scared me. I thought in a way that he was possessed and that maybe from then on he always would be.

Everybody came to our house to eat. I just sat in the bedroom by myself. My uncle opened the door and said, "You okay?"

I said, "I'm fine," and then I burst into tears. He let himself in and listened to me cry. I told him my horrible secret that I had told myself I would never tell anyone and that I had made Sammy promise never to tell. But now I started to blabber. "Uncle, sometimes while Lynn was sick, I got angry at her. Usually I hid it from her, but one time I got mad out loud. It was the middle of the night, and she asked me for a glass of milk. I got up and got her the milk, but when she tasted it, she said she didn't want it and dropped it on the floor. She got to acting like that when she didn't feel well. Then I brought her water and started to clean up the milk. But she said the water glass had soap on it, so she threw it on the floor, too. Then she said she wanted milk again, and I wouldn't get her any. She said she hated me, and I told her I hated her. I made her cry. Uncle, what's wrong with me?" I sobbed some more. "How come I said I hated her?" I tried to inhale, but the air didn't seem to go into my lungs. I struggled to breathe.

Uncle let me sob for a few minutes. Then he said, "Did anyone ever tell you that my first son died?"

I stopped crying for a moment. "Really? I didn't know you had another son."

"He was just a baby. You weren't even born yet, and neither was Lynn."

"Was that a baby from your first wife?"

"Oh, no, I was only married to her for a few months," he said. "This was Fumi's first baby. The baby was born very sick. Fumi or I

221

sat with him every night. All he did night after night was cry, until the day he died. He was quiet that day."

"I'm sorry. I'm so sorry, Uncle."

"I know you are. That's not why I'm telling you. I just want you to know I understand. Lynnie didn't hate you. You didn't hate Lynnie. You were mad because she was so sick. There was one day when my son was so sick and in such pain, I thought I should just smother him with a pillow to take him out of his misery."

"But that's terrible!"

"Of course it is. I didn't do it. I would never do it. When someone is dying, you have crazy thoughts. Don't feel guilty, you're too young for that."

Then he told me that some Buddhists believe the spirit leaves the earth forty-nine days after the body dies. He said for the next forty-nine days I could stay busy by taking care of a box of Lynn's things he would help me make. He said this box would be Lynn's altar. He started to leave, but I called out, "Uncle Katsuhisa!"

"What is it, sweetheart?"

"Are you happy now? I don't mean today, I mean in general."

He paused, and I could see he was really thinking. He turned both of his ears inside out at the same time. *Pop! Pop!* "Yes, I would say that, all in all, today I'm a happy man. It's not always easy, but, yes, I am."

A week after the funeral I turned in my new essay at school. This is what I wrote:

Here is a special memory about my sister, Lynn. One day in Iowa there was a strong wind, the kind of wind that seems to go up and down and back and forth. I could hardly see because my hair was blowing around my face. Some of the corn blew almost flat. Lynn and I climbed on a ladder to the top of the roof with two boxes of Kleenex. She said to take the Kleenex out one at a time and let the wind catch it. In a few minutes hundreds of tissues sailed over the cornfield. I held the hair out of my eyes to watch. The tissues looked like giant butterflies.

Later we got in trouble, and our allowance was docked for the price of the Kleenex. We had to go and pick up every single piece. It was worth it to see the butterflies flying over the corn.

Lynn could take a simple, everyday object like a box of Kleenex and use it to prove how amazing the world is. She could prove this in many different ways, with Kleenex or soap bubbles or maybe even a blade of grass. This is the main theme of my sister's life.

chapter 16

きらきら

WE MADE LYNN'S altar on her desk, facing
the big magnolia, which kept its leaves all winter. Uncle made me a beautiful wooden box in
which I placed her chewed-up pencil, a lock of
her hair my mother had cut, her toenail clip-
pings, and other really sacred items like that.
He'd even inserted a piece of removable glass
in the wood under which I could place a picture of Lynn. I started to make our daily rice
instead of my mother, and I put a bowl of fresh
rice out every day for Lynn. I also kept her
favorite water glass full. Sometimes I gave her

milk and treats. Other times I would have a feeling that she might want fresh air, so I would open the window over her desk.

My mother and father became like zombies. They ate but didn't seem to taste their food. They slept but never deeply—I often heard them get up in the middle of the night. During the days we talked to one another but without joy. Sometimes I felt they were even disappointed in me because I wasn't Lynn. Other times they got the "We should haves": "We should have fed her liver from when she was younger"; "We should have taken her to that doctor in Chicago"; "We should have tried to buy a house sooner."

Every day for dinner my mother fed us either SPAM and rice or sardines and rice. The dishes piled up. It looked as if we might lose the house because my parents still owed money on Lynn's medical bills and my mother wouldn't work as many hours any longer. I think she felt there was no reason to work hard anymore.

I got so sick of sardines and SPAM that I started to make dinner for the family. The first five nights I made my favorite dinner: ramen noodles with fish cakes and green onion. The sixth through tenth nights I made my second favorite dinner: pizza. Ramen and pizza were the end of my repertoire. Every night after dinner I washed the dishes and cleaned the counters with a new sponge my father had bought me. I did all this so that my mother wouldn't go insane over how messy the kitchen was getting.

My mother, already thin, still cried all the time and lost weight. My father grew thin, and his skin became waxy and pale. I needed to fatten them up. I borrowed a cookbook from Mrs. Kanagawa and made a different dinner every night.

On the forty-ninth day after Lynn's death I opened all the windows in the alcove, even though it was raining. I closed my eyes and tried to feel Lynn's spirit. A leaf suddenly fell off the magnolia tree and flew in the wind and hit the screen right in front of me. I believed that leaf was a sign from Lynn.

When she first died, I felt sorry about all the pills I'd given her that made her feel so miserable. But now I didn't feel so many regrets. Lynn wanted her life. I thought she was willing to suffer if she could still taste her food, if she could still talk about the sea, if she could still feel a breeze across her face, and even if she could still argue with her crazy sister!

I cried and cried. But then I had to stop. One thing about me was that when I was having a serious wish session, I tried never to wish impossible wishes. I might have wished for sixteen crayons instead of eight, but even when I was little, I never wished for a thousand crayons, because I knew a thousand different crayons did not exist. So on that forty-ninth day I did not wish that Lynn could be alive again, because I knew she was gone. I was worried that her spirit was watching me every time I cried. I was worried that if she saw me crying, she would be very unhappy and maybe she wouldn't be able to leave the earth the way she was supposed to. So even though I wanted her to keep watching me, I wished she would forget about me and never see me crying and never worry about me anymore, even if that meant I was now alone.

I worked harder at school, because that was one of Lynn's last wishes. It was pretty boring. I hoped Lynn wasn't watching me, but just in case she was, I spent a lot of time on my homework. The first time I got an A on a math test, my parents were so surprised and proud, they found a frame and hung up the test in their bedroom. That A actually brought a bit of life into their eyes. They mentioned it to everyone they talked to. It was strange to see them so excited about one A, since Lynnie had gotten a zillion of them.

Sometimes, no matter how hard I tried, I got a C. That happened a lot. But when I worked hard, I got better grades. This surprised me. I guess because Lynn was so smart and it had seemed easy for her to get good grades, I never noticed how hard she worked. I thought getting an A was something that happened to you, not something you made happen. But after Lynn had died and I'd spent a lot of time think-ing about her, I remembered how often I'd seen her sitting at her desk, chewing her pencil as she worked for hours on her homework.

When summer came, I turned twelve. For my birthday my father took Silly and me down to Lynnie's grave. We cleaned the grave and planted some flowers. Then we did a dance in our persona as the Shirondas. We'd been practicing almost every day in preparation for performing for Lynn. Silly was Wanda Shironda, and I was Rhonda Shironda. We knew all the words to quite a few songs, and we had worked out some special dance steps just for today. My father watched proudly while we performed "Hit the Road, Jack," "Where the Boys Are," "Will You Love Me Tomorrow?" and "Twisting the Night Away." He even laughed a little. That little bit of laughing changed him. He seemed surprised that he could still laugh.

When we got home, he walked into my bedroom and just stared at Lynn's bed. Then he said, "I guess you and Sammy need more room in here. Why don't you help me?" My father's eyes filled with tears as he and I lifted Lynn's mattress and bedspring out of the room. We didn't throw them away, though. We called Uncle to ask him to store her bed in his attic.

When Uncle came for the bed, I heard him say to my father that Mr. Lyndon was not going to give the factory workers a raise that year. I said, "Why not bash his car again?" Uncle and my father looked at me, then at each other, and then at me again.

When Uncle Katsuhisa had left, my father told me to get in the car. My mother was sitting with Sammy in the living room.

"What about me?" said Sammy.

"Just Katie," said my father.

We got in the car and drove and drove. Eventually, my father turned up a long private road, a road I'd traveled on once before with him. Mr. Lyndon's mansion rose in the distance. My heart sank. I thought my father was going to bash another car.

"Dad!" I said. "I'm sorry I said you should bash his car again!"

He said, "We're going to apologize for what I did to Mr. Lyndon's car."

That seemed just as bad to me. "Apologize! But he doesn't know it was you! Dad! He doesn't even know. You don't have to apologize." He looked at me as if he was very disappointed I'd said that. I didn't care. I just wanted to protect my father. "Dad, you'll get in trouble!"

He parked close to the front of the mansion. When I got out of the car, the house seemed as big as a castle. It was so big and beautiful, it made me gasp. It seemed a thousand people could live in that one house.

"Everyone says Mr. Lyndon is mean," I said.

"I believe I've heard that too."

My father rapped hard on the front door. It was the most exquisite door I'd ever seen. Roses and vines were carved into the rich wood. A maid opened up. She wore a little outfit just like the maids I'd seen on TV. She was very beautiful. Her skin was the same color as my brown silk hat my mother had made me for my birthday.

"Hello!" I said, surprised.

"Hello!" she said, equally surprised.

My father said, "I'm the man who wrecked Mr. Lyndon's car. I've come to apologize."

The maid hesitated. "Wait here, sir." She closed the exquisite door.

"Dad, you didn't really wreck it."

He didn't answer. We stood looking not at each other, but at the door. The door opened again. "Come in," the maid said.

She led us to a room and directed us to sit on a couch covered in plastic. The ceiling, which was twice as high as the ceiling in our house, was painted blue like the sky, and there were clouds and angels.

Mr. Lyndon came in. My father and I stood up. Mr. Lyndon was big, and he looked as if he may have been strong when he was young. But now he was old. His chin jutted out, and his face was cracked like a field suffering from drought. Two gray dogs followed Mr. Lyndon in. They growled but didn't move from Mr. Lyndon's side. They sat when he sat. We sat too. Mr. Lyndon looked right at me! It was as if he didn't even notice my father was in the room. Mr. Lyndon gestured toward a bowl of candy on the table.

"Take all you want, young lady."

I took a lemon drop, even though I didn't like them. "Thank you," I said.

"Take more!" he bellowed.

I took two more.

"Go on, eat them!"

I put all three of them into my mouth. That seemed to satisfy Mr. Lyndon, who turned to my father and waited.

"I'm the man who wrecked your car," said my father. "I wanted to apologize. My daughter died that day, and I wasn't myself."

"Are you one of my sexers, Mr. . . . ?"

I could see the question annoyed my father, but I didn't know why. "I'm one of *the* sexers," said my father. "I'm Masao Takeshima."

"I'm very sorry about your daughter. Another of my sexers lost a child once, and he didn't wreck my car. You won't be returning to work in my hatchery."

I wondered if the worker he referred to was my uncle.

If my father was surprised, he didn't show it. He said, "I'm going to reimburse you."

Mr. Lyndon stood up. "Of course you are. You'll hear from my attorney."

I started to stand up but remained seated because my father did. The backs of my legs were already sweaty from sitting on the plastic covering the couch. The lemon drops made me thirsty. Then when my father stood up, I did too. I saw my father was not intimidated by Mr. Lyndon. And that was how I learned that even when you're very, very wrong, if you apologize, you can still hold yourself with dignity. "Good-bye, Mr. Lyndon," my father said. We walked out.

When we got into our car, I saw the maid peeking out the front window. She waved slightly, and I waved slightly back. Before he started the car, my father said, "I don't ever want you to be afraid to apologize."

I said, "Dad, you don't have a job!"

"I still have the other hatchery," he said. He thought a moment. "I've heard there's an opening at a hatchery in Missouri. If it's time to move on, it's time to move on."

Missouri! We didn't speak again. I saw that my father was a little shaken up over being fired, but at the same time he didn't seem to regret apologizing.

He ended up getting a job at one of the few hatcheries in the state that wasn't owned by Mr. Lyndon. He had to drive a little farther, unfortunately. But he never complained. I think that summer, when my father moved Lynnie's bed, and when he went to apologize to Mr. Lyndon, he'd realized that we had a choice: Either we could be an unhappy family forever, or not.

At the end of the summer Silly's mother held a pro-union meeting at her house. Surprisingly, my parents let me go to her house to help out. Mrs. Kilgore came and picked me up. Silly and I made snacks for everyone. We cut up carrots and celery and made onion dip with sour cream and Lipton soup mix. About a hundred people showed up. They didn't fit into the house, so the meeting was held outside and the snacks were inside.

About halfway through the meeting I was shocked when my parents arrived. They must have left Sammy with Mrs. Kanagawa. They barely acknowledged me. They listened quietly to the last few speakers.

My parents left before me. I wondered whether I'd imagined they were there. When I got home later, my mother said nothing about the union. She was dusting Lynn's altar, even though the forty-nine days had passed and Lynn had already left the earth. My mother didn't look up as she dusted. "What was wrong with that little girl in the blue dress?" she said.

"The one with no hair?"

"Yes." She opened the window slightly.

"Mrs. Kilgore says she has cancer." My mother didn't answer. "Mom?"

"Yes, dear."

"The union wants to give the factory workers three days off with pay for grief leave, like if a family member dies."

She pursed her lips and looked at me severely. "It's a little late for that," she said.

My mother didn't say anything more. But when the union vote was held the next week, the union won by one vote. That was a surprise, because everyone had expected it to lose by one vote. My mother seemed pleased that the union had won, so I knew how she'd voted. I don't think it was any of the speeches she'd heard that made her vote for the union.

Before Lynn died, my mother would have done anything for her own family, but she would not have done much for another family. I think it was a combination of Lynn dying and seeing the little girl in the blue dress that changed my mother's vote. It was a little late for my mother, but if she voted yes, she knew it would not be too late for the next family suffering grief.

At the local recreation center Silly and I performed as the Shirondas in the annual fall talent show. We came in twelfth out of twenty, which of course I thought was a tremendous injustice. Every afternoon we practiced for the next year's show. Every night at home I cooked for my family, and every day at school I got more B's and sometimes even an A. Sometimes the thought of Lynn and how smart she was made us proud and even happy instead of unhappy. Sometimes seeing a picture of her could fill us with joyful memories instead of only sad ones. We were still paying medical bills, but we were making progress.

When the holidays came around, the house grew glum. Whenever I felt glum, I started to wonder why it mattered whether I got an A, a B, or a C. My father felt bad for me and asked whether I wanted to take a vacation.

"Yeah!" I said. "I mean, yes, yes, yes!"

"Would you like to go see the Okefenokee Swamp?"

"How about California? That's what Lynnie would have wanted."

"Why do you think that?"

"Because that's where the sea she loved is. That's where she wanted to live when she got older."

He said he would think about it.

After Christmas he announced that he was going to take us to California for vacation.

Before we left, my father and I stopped by my sister's grave. My mother did not come because she could not bear to.

My father had taken off only two days of work when Lynn died. We were trying to survive back then. He needed to buy food for me and Sammy, so he could not spend all his time crying. I know that sounds coldhearted, but it was not. He needed to think about his children who were still alive, because he was honor-bound to think of the living before the dead. If he stopped working for three days, that might mean we would not eat fish one night or could not pay the mortgage on what we thought of as Lynn's house.

At the grave site my father cleaned off Lynnie's small stone and laid down a bunch of white flowers. He said, "I remember when a twelve-year-old could run away and make a good life. That's what I should have done when I was a boy. I almost did." I knew he couldn't remember such a time, only thought he could, because he'd told me how when he was twelve, he and Uncle Katuhisa had needed to stop their education in Japan and return to California to help their parents on the family farm. So he only thought that everything could have happened differently, if only he had started life a little differently.

He said now that maybe if he'd set off at twelve, he would have ended up staying in California instead of going to Iowa with his family. Since more Japanese people lived in

California than in Iowa, when he and my mother eventually opened a grocery store, it would have stayed in business. Then maybe they would have had more money, and when they had Lynn, maybe she would have been healthier. This, of course, was impossible, for he had met my mother in Iowa, not in California. If he'd stayed in California, he wouldn't have met her and Lynn wouldn't have been born. But I didn't say this. I didn't say anything because I could see he really felt like imagining what might have happened, if only.

It was during this trip to the cemetery that my father mentioned to me that Lynn had wanted me to have her diary. Later, after we got home, I sat in my tiny old bedroom and read it straight through. The windows were closed, but I pulled my sweater tightly around myself. I loved our house, but it was drafty at night.

I'd always thought of Lynn's handwriting as consistent and perfect and even kind of majestic. In her diary I saw that sometimes she wrote messier than other times. Like when she was excited about Gregg, her penmanship grew rushed and even sloppy, for her. I was the only person she mentioned every single day, even if she just wrote something like, *Katie got another C today*. Her handwriting wavered toward the end, especially at the very end. Here is her last diary entry:

Dear Diary,

To my parents I leave the contents of my bank account, $5.47.

To Sammy I leave the two one-dollar bills hidden in my top left desk drawer. I also leave him all my toys and the candy bar in my bottom right desk drawer.

To Katie I leave my diary, my dictionary, and my encyclopedia, which she had better use.

Signed,
Lynn Akiko Takeshima

She wrote this four days before she died. Four days before she died, I'd still had hope that she would get better. My parents said they didn't give me the diary when Lynn died because they thought it would be too upsetting for me. It was odd to hear them say that, because I'd thought it was I who'd taken care of them after Lynn died. But they seemed to think that *they* had taken care of me.

My own handwriting was as messy as ever. I didn't care because someday, when I went to college, I would use a typewriter.

We drove to California near the end of the month. When we arrived, on December 31, it was eighty-five degrees, and the Santa Ana winds whipped against the rickety walls of our motel room. A single cricket chirped in the bathroom all night. During the day several crows cawed at us when we walked to our car. Lynnie had always thought crickets and even crows were good luck. Now and then I thought I heard Lynn's lively voice. The cricket sang, "Chirp! Chirp!" but I heard *"Kira-kira!"* The crows called "Caw! Caw!" and I heard *"Kira-kira!"* The wind whistled "Whoosh! Whoosh!" and I heard *"Kira-kira!"* My sister had taught me to look at the world that way, as a place that glitters, as a place where the calls of the crickets and the crows and the wind are everyday occurrences that also happen to be magic.

I wished Lynn could have lived to see the sea with us! When we first walked up to the Pacific Ocean, the tears welled up in my eyes and her death seemed near. I don't think anyone understood as well as I did how badly Lynn had longed to walk along the water the way my family and I did that New Year's Day. I hid my tears from my parents. But the water started to make me feel happy again. Here at the sea—especially at the sea—I could hear my sister's voice in the waves: *"Kira-kira! Kira-kira!"*

Reading Group Guide

Kira-Kira
By Cynthia Kadohata

Prereading Activity

Kira-kira means "glittering" in Japanese. Ask students to write a one-page description of something that is *kira-kira* to them. Examples may include the ocean, stars, the moon, the morning dew on the grass, a dancer under a spotlight, etc. Invite them to share their writing in class.

Discussion Questions

• Mrs. Takeshima is troubled at how "un-Japanese" her daughters seem, and vows to one day send them back to Japan. Debate how difficult it was in the early 1950s to belong to one culture and live in another. Why is Mrs. Takeshima so fearful that her daughters will lose their sense of heritage? Discuss customs that the Takeshima family practices that demonstrates the family's loyalty to their native culture.

• Katie describes her mother as "a delicate, rare, and beautiful flower." Find examples in the novel that support Katie's description of her mother.

• Discuss Katie and Lynn's relationship. Why does Katie feel that her parents like Lynn best? It is Lynn who tells Katie that they are moving to

Georgia, and it is Lynn who tells her that their mother is pregnant. Why do Mr. and Mrs. Takeshima leave such important discussions up to Lynn? At what point do Lynn and Katie switch roles?

• Describe the friendship that develops between Lynn and Amber. What does Katie mean when she says, "Amber broke ranks and became Lynn's first best friend"? Why does Amber drop Lynn as a friend? Discuss why Katie is so hurt that Amber doesn't come to Lynn's funeral. Contrast Katie and Silly's friendship with Lynn and Amber's.

• What is Uncle Katsuhisa's role in the family? *Katsu* means "triumph" in Japanese. How does Uncle Katsuhisa live up to his name? Katie finds it difficult to see that her father and uncle are brothers. Contrast their personalities. What does Mrs. Takeshima mean when she says that Uncle Katsuhisa "didn't look before he leapt"?

• Hitting, stealing, and lying are the three worst crimes to Mr. and Mrs. Takeshima. How does Katie commit each of these crimes in the course of the novel? Discuss the scene where Katie steals pink nail polish for Lynn. How does she justify this crime to herself? Discuss why Katie's crime makes her mother feel that the family is falling apart.

• Lynn wakes up crying one night and says that in her dream she is swimming in the ocean. How does this dream foreshadow her death? Discuss the symbolism of the brown moth in Lynn's bedroom on the night she dies.

• Describe the sense of community among the Japanese families in Chesterfield, Georgia. Mr. Kanagawa is considered the leader of the community. How is his leadership revealed in the novel? How does Lynn become the leader of the children in the community?

• Prejudice is an underlying theme in the novel. The first time that Katie experiences prejudice is at the motel in Tennessee when her family is moving to Georgia. Why does Mr. Takeshima quietly give in to the motel clerk and take the room in the back? How does Lynn help Katie understand the prejudices that she will experience at school? Discuss why the Japanese mothers cut and curl their daughters' hair when they begin school. Debate whether they really believe that changing the girls' appearances will make them fit in, and suffer less acts of prejudice.

• Discuss the meaning of the word *exploit*. How does Mr. Lyndon exploit the workers at the hatchery? Some of the workers are trying to unionize so that they can demand better working conditions. Mrs. Takeshima stays away from them because she feels that it is wrong to fight the people who are trying to help you. Why does she feel that Mr. Lyndon is trying to help them?

Why do Mr. and Mrs. Takeshima decide to attend the pro-union meeting at the end of the novel?

• Discuss how the trip to California helps Katie come to terms with Lynn's death. How does she help her parents deal with their grief?

• What are the elements of hope in the novel?

Research and Activities

• Mrs. Takeshima feels that her girls must return to Japan to learn about their femininity. Research the role of women in Japan today. Write a brief article that might appear in a book called *Women in Other Cultures*.

• Brenda Swamp, named for a ten-year-old girl who died there, is near Chesterfield, Georgia, and is the subject of a local ghost story. Write and illustrate a story titled "Brenda" that Katie might one day read to Sammy.

• Katie has to answer three questions about a story her class reads. Apply the same questions to *Kira-Kira* and write the answers in three paragraphs:
    • What is the author trying to say in the scene where Mr. Takeshima confesses to Mr. Lyndon that he bashed his car?

    • What is the theme of the story?

- How does the main character change at the end of the novel?

- Katie notices that her parents work all the time and never take time to relax and have fun. Research the ritual of the Japanese tea ceremony (known as *chanoyu* or *chado*). Plan a tea ceremony that Katie might have for her parents.

- Katie gives one of the eulogies at Lynn's funeral but sits down before she tells a special memory of Lynn. Write about a special memory of Lynn that Katie might have included in the eulogy.

- Silly Kilgore's mother holds a pro-union meeting at her house at the end of the summer. Have the class plan this meeting. Instruct the speakers to point out the poor working conditions, long hours, safety issues, and low pay. Such meetings are only for the workers, but suggest that one student give a speech from Katie Takeshima's point of view.

- Lynn always wanted to go to the ocean in California. Write a haiku titled "Kira-Kira" that Katie might create and dedicate to Lynn after her family returns from the West Coast.

- It is a Japanese custom to purchase souvenirs (or *omiyage*) from places they have traveled. Write a description of a souvenir that Katie might bring from California to put at Lynn's grave.

CHAPTER ONE

Kouun is "good luck" in Japanese, and one year my family had none of it. We were cursed with bad luck. Bad luck chased us around, pointing her bony finger. We got seven flat tires in six weeks. I got malaria, one of fifteen hundred cases in the United States that year. And my grandmother's spine started causing her excruciating pain.

Furthermore, random bad smells emanated from we knew not where. And my brother, Jaz, became cursed with invisibility. Nobody noticed him except us. His best friend had moved away, and he did not know a single boy to hang around with. Even our cousins looked the other way when they saw him at our annual Christmas party. They didn't even seem to be snubbing my brother; they just didn't see him.

The thing about luck is that it's like a fever. You can take fever meds and lie in bed and drink chicken broth and sleep seventeen hours in a row, but basically your fever will break when it wants to break.

In early April my parents got a call from Japan. Three elderly relatives were getting ready to die and wanted my parents to take care of them in their last weeks and months. There was nothing surprising about this. This was just the way our year was going. It was April 25 when my grandparents and Jaz delivered my parents to the airport to catch their plane to Japan. I stayed at home because the type of malaria I'd gotten was called "airport malaria." Airport malaria is when a rogue mosquito from, say, Africa has been inadvertently carried into the United States on a jet. This infected mosquito might bite you. I got bit in Florida last summer, and I lived in Kansas. The chances that I would get malaria from going to the airport in Kansas were remote, but I'd grown so scared of mosquitoes that sometimes I didn't even like stepping outside. It really wasn't fair—I was only twelve, and yet already I was scared of the entire outside world.

During the 1940s there were thousands of malaria cases in the United States. Then in the fifties the experts thought malaria here was eradicated. But every so often, someone still caught it. Sometimes you would get your picture in the newspaper. My picture was even in *Time* magazine!

Obaachan and Jiichan, my grandmother and grandfather on my mother's side, were both sixty-seven and lived with us in Littlefield, Kansas. "Obaachan" was more formal than "Baachan," but it was what she wanted Jaz and me to call her.

When harvest season arrived in May of our horrible year, Jiichan planned to come out of retirement to work as a combine driver for a custom harvesting company called Parker Harvesting, Inc. (I'll explain about custom harvesting in a minute or two.) My grandmother would work as a cook for the same harvester, with me as her helper.

We'd all worked for the Parkers before. But it was the first time my parents wouldn't be there, which meant only my grandparents would be paying the mortgage during harvest this year. I didn't quite understand what "paying the mortgage" meant, but apparently, it was a constant struggle. Another phrase that came up a lot was "paying down the principal," as in, "If we could just pay down the principal, I'd feel like we were getting somewhere." I used to think that "paying down the principal" meant they wanted to bribe the principal at one of my future schools, like they would give this principal some money, and then someday the principal would let me into high school despite my iffy grades.

Anyway. As soon as my grandparents got home from dropping off my parents, changes were implemented. My mother had told Jaz, "Don't worry. You'll make a friend when you least expect it." My grandparents were more proactive. It seems Obaachan and Jiichan had a bright idea they'd been hiding from us.

Obaachan made Jaz and me sit on the floor in front of the coffee table while she and Jiichan sat on the couch. "We having meeting-party," she announced regally. "We invite boys we will consider for friendship with Jaz." She turned to me. "Make list with him. I no interfere."

"A list of people to invite?" I asked. My Doberman, Thunder, tried to push himself between me and the table. I pushed back, and we just sat there, leaning hard into each other.

"No! A list!" she snapped at me.

Wasn't that what I had just said? I finally got up and moved to a different side of the table. Still unsure what she wanted, I got a pen and paper.

"Pencil! You may need to erase."

I got a pencil and readied myself. "Should I number the list?" I asked.

My grandfather nodded sagely. "Agenda," he said. "List for boys we invite, agenda for party."

"No interfere!" Obaachan said to Jiichan.

"You interfere first!"

"No!"

Obaachan and Jiichan had been married for forty-nine years, and my mother always said that after that number of years, you no longer had to be polite all the time. It sometimes seemed that in our house, I was the only one who had to use my manners. Jaz didn't have to because he had issues. When I'm sixty-seven, in fifty-five years, I supposed that I would finally be able to dispense with my manners.

I thought Jiichan and Obaachan talked to each other the way that they did because they'd had an arranged marriage. Obaachan said that if I had an arranged marriage, I would never give or receive a broken heart. If I grew up beautiful, I would never break any man's heart, and if I grew up plain, nobody would break my heart. If I rebelled and wanted love, however, all bets were off. Broken hearts would come my way like locusts.

"Summer! You in rah-rah land." She never said "la-la land," and I never corrected her.

I hurriedly wrote *Number one* on the paper in the left-hand margin.

"No number," Obaachan said. "Arrange by time. I have to tell you everything?"

Jiichan picked up the paper, studied the *Number one*, and set the paper back down. "I agree. Arrange by time."

I erased the *Number one* and wrote in *One o'clock p.m.* I made sure not to flick the eraser bits onto the floor, because if I did, Obaachan would be so upset that she might fall over dead.

"Noon!" barked Obaachan. I made the change. "Continue. First write day on top of paper in big letter. Day for meeting is next Saturday. Then continue."

"What would you like to do at noon?" I asked Jaz.

"Play with LEGOs. I want a LEGO party."

"Not really party," Jiichan said. He was cleaning his teeth with the floss he always carried in his shirt pocket. Sometimes he flossed during dinner, right at the table. See what I mean about manners? Can you imagine what your parents would do if you started to floss at the dinner table? But he constantly seemed to have something between his teeth. "More of meeting than party," he said.

"Noon lunchtime," Obaachan said. "You feed boys first. Boys always hungry. Never mind. I no interfere. But no food, no friend. What I just say?"

"No food, no friend," Jaz and I repeated.

Obaachan sometimes made us repeat something she had just said, to prove we were listening.

Jaz turned to Obaachan. "Obaachan, will you make sandwiches?"

"Summer make. I her mentor."

I found myself already starting to feel stressed. What if I made ham sandwiches and the boys wanted tuna fish? What if I used regular bread and one of the boys needed gluten-free, like my friend Alyssa had to eat because of her allergies? What if I used too much mayonnaise? Arghhh!

Still, next to *Noon* I wrote *Sandwich eating*.

Jiichan pounded on the paper. "Lunch!" he cried out passionately. "Not 'sandwich eating'! It called 'lunch'!" He clutched at his heart. "You kids go to kill me." Apparently, about once every couple of weeks, he thought we were going to kill him.

"What kind of sandwiches would you like?" I asked Jaz, still worrying about those. "I don't want to make the wrong kind."

"I'll ask around at school. I can't believe this is happening. I'm really going to have a meeting-party." He got up to look at himself in a mirror over our fake fireplace and said, "You are going to have a meeting-party."

Jiichan was now standing and staggering away from us with his hands on his heart. Jaz and I watched him calmly. "I die, scatter ashes," Jiichan said. "No keep in hole in wall at cemetery. You hear me?"

"Yes, Jiichan," we said.

"Good. Then I die happy."

I wrote down *LEGOs, one o'clock.* My brother had approximately one thousand dollars' worth of LEGOs. Seriously. I counted once. LEGOs were one of our biggest expenses and the only thing we splurged on.

"Good plan!" Jiichan said. "That brilliant!" I couldn't tell if he was being sarcastic as he peered over my shoulder from his death throes.

"How long is the meeting-party?" Jaz asked.

"I think most parties are two hours," I answered. "So I guess that's the end of the agenda?" Nobody answered, so I made a line underneath the agenda and laid down the pencil.

"Who should I invite?" Jaz asked. "Should it be just kids who I think might come, or should it be kids who might not come but on the other hand you never know? Should it be just kids in my class, or should it be all the kids in my grade? Should it be boys and girls or just boys? Should it be only kids who might not even know who I am even though I know who they are? Should it—"

Jiichan held up his palm to quiet Jaz. "Invite whole fifth grade," he said wisely. We all looked at him, and he nodded. "That way hurt nobody's feelings."

Jaz stared at him doubtfully for a moment, but then his face turned from doubtful to ecstatic. I could almost hear him thinking, *Wow, the whole school might come to my meeting-party!*

Then my grandparents wanted Jaz to draw invitations. He was a good artist in kind of a weird way. Like, he never drew pictures of anything recognizable, but if you needed a totally psychedelic design, he was your man. But he wanted to buy invitations because he thought they were more official. We ended up driving thirty miles to a 99-cent store in a larger town. After loud and passionate debate, we bought several boxes of dinosaur invitations. On Monday,

Jaz distributed them to all the kids in the fifth grade at his school.

So as not to jinx the party, we weren't supposed to talk to one another about it. But we could pray all we wanted, in front of several sprigs of silk cherry blossoms on the coffee table. We did this the night before the party. Cherry blossoms, as the harbingers of spring, were important to Japanese farmers. My grandmother mumbled in Japanese as I knelt beside her. I could make out a word occasionally—like *unmei* for "destiny."

As Obaachan muttered on, I prayed in my head: *Please let my brother have a successful meeting-party. Let the kids have fun, let him make at least one friend, preferably two. Please, please, please.*

That night I drew in my notebook like I always did. I didn't draw very well, so each picture took me weeks. I copied them from photographs of mosquitoes I found.

One time I thought I had a perfect drawing, so I sent it to a mosquito expert, and this is what he said: "Looks like an Anopheles, but the proboscis is 'hairy' and the palps look like a thin line, so this is not a good representation, but could easily be changed (make palps more than a line and get rid of bristle on mouthparts and you have an Anopheles female). The problem is that most (but not all) Anopheles in the U.S. tend to have spots on their wings, which these drawings lack." Wow, epic fail on my part!

It was strange because I knew that if I had almost been killed by a car, I wouldn't have become fascinated with cars. If I had almost drowned, I wouldn't have become obsessed with water. But the more I looked at mosquitoes, even the same type that had infected me, the more delicate they seemed. Fragile, even. And yet one had almost taken my life. It was like now we couldn't be separated. I mean, if I saw one on my arm, I wouldn't hesitate to smash it or even run screaming down the highway. They terrified me. But still, we were inseparable.